EVERYTHING THAT'S UNDERNEATH

KRISTI DEMEESTER

"Kristi DeMeester's wonderfully disturbing *Everything That's Underneath* features a cast of characters who are as emotionally raw and authentic as they are haunted. DeMeester's mothers and daughters, struggling at the edges of a society/economy as cold and uncaring as the universe, succumb in the face of horrors made even more terrifying by their nagging sense of familiarity. A dark, intelligent, relentless collection."
— Paul Tremblay, author of *A Head Full of Ghosts* and *Disappearance at Devil's Rock*

"In *Everything That's Underneath*, Kristi DeMeester lays out a series of evocative visions and bizarre terrors that deftly meld the gothic, religious, and darkly fantastic to tell tales of body horror and transformation. Her fiction explores the ways we are often betrayed by our flesh and led astray by our own desires. DeMeester is a rising star of weird horror, and this debut collection is evidence that her transformative visions are destined to leave their mark."
— Simon Strantzas, author of *Burnt Black Suns*

"With these stories Kristi DeMeester conjures earthy magic out of seemingly ordinary circumstances. Her characters, through ritual and instinct, discover a rough connection to all living things, but that connection may not bring comfort. This is DeMeester's particular brand of cosmic horror, coming from deep down in the bones, imbued with animal vitality and ingrained wisdom. She's bringing themes of every day life, including love and domestic violence, to a much larger canvas and simultaneously taking nature at large to a deeply personal level. The effects are uncanny and unsettling. A young writer, Demeester is already established as a talent to watch in horror and weird fiction. I look forward to more of these dark, fierce, disturbing tales."

Apex Publications, LLC, PO Box 24323, Lexington, KY 40524

ISBN 978-1-937009-57-1

"Everything That's Underneath" —previously published in *Nightscript 1*

"The Wicked Shall Come Upon Him" —previously published in *Cthulusattva: Tales From the Black Gnosis*

"To Sleep Long, to Sleep Deep" —previously published in *Jamais Vu*

"The Fleshtival" —previously published in *Strange Aeons*

"The Beautiful Nature of Venom" —previously published in *Pank! Magazine*

"Like Feather, Like Bone" —previously published in *Shimmer, Year's Best Weird Fiction Vol. 1*, and *Great Jones Street*

"Worship Only What She Bleeds" —original

"The Tying of Tongues" —previously published in *Daily Science Fiction*

"The Marking" —previously published in *Three-Lobed Burning Eye* and *Year's Best Weird Fiction Vol. 3*

"The Long Road" —previously published in *Shock Totem*

"The Lightning Bird" —original

"The Dream Eater" —previously published in *Split Tongues*, a limited chapbook from Dim Shores

"Daughters of Hecate" —previously published in *Xnoybis 2* and *Great Jones Street*

"Birthright" —original novelette

"All That Is Refracted, Broken" —previously published in *LampLight*

"December Skin" —previously published in *Black Static*

"Split Tongues" —previously published in *Split Tongues,* a limited chapbook from Dim Shores

"To Sleep in the Dust of the Earth"—previously published in *Shimmer* and translated in *Zwielicht*

For the two Js. As Always.

Everything That's Underneath

Carin left the door ajar for Benjamin. He'd come inside only once that day smelling of sawdust and ice and swallowed the sandwich she'd made for him, pecked her on the cheek, and returned to his project. When he went, cold air swirled through the kitchen and caught at her hair and cheeks, and she stilled her hands which reached to grasp the shoulders of his coat.

"A door," he'd told her.

"We have a door."

"No. Something solid. Something good," he'd said.

The next week he'd rented a saw, borrowed a truck from Tom next door, and dragged home a pile of lumber. At night, the smell of cedar leaked inside of her, and she dreamed of great trees, tangles of limbs and roots reaching deep into the earth under a blood red sky. Redwoods and oaks and cedars wrapping tight around her body, squeezing until she fought for breath. Her ribs and sternum cracking under the impossible weight.

"I don't like the smell," she'd told him that morning, watching the liquid movements of his body as he pulled on his thermals and boots. Every movement calculated and precise.

She'd fallen in love with him while watching those delicate hands fold and unfold a napkin.

When was the last time he'd danced? She couldn't remember.

Even that was a lie. Of all the things she'd learned to believe these past three months, this was the easiest.

"Everyone likes the smell. It keeps moths away."

"I guess I don't."

"It won't be as strong once it's done. You won't even notice it."

"Sure."

"Don't come out, okay? I want it to be a surprise."

For hours that day, she'd stood at the kitchen window, her hand against the glass, listening to the sharp bite of metal against wood. The sound of her husband slowly, carefully putting it together again.

Something solid. Something good.

Outside, full dark had fallen, and still the saw whined.

Surely a door was a fairly simple thing? Benjamin was no carpenter, but he'd watched videos online, read articles, and it seemed easy enough. A Saturday project. Something he could finish in one day, maybe two if he ran into any snags or really screwed something up.

He'd hidden himself behind the large shed in their backyard. When the realtor had shown them the house, Benjamin had turned to her and smiled, slow and quiet. The secret smile he kept just for her. His lips mouthing the word "studio." They'd put an offer on the house that afternoon. He'd just started the renovations when his vision began to blur and his toes had started to tingle and go numb.

Now and then she would see the top of his hat or a sudden dervish of sawdust caught in the air, but she never actually saw *him*. She tried not to worry. The doctors had said his prognosis was good, that he should be able to carry on as normal with a few slight modifications. That she shouldn't feel the need to hover over him, waiting and watching for another day like the one where she'd found him on the floor of the shed, shaking and whispering that he couldn't feel his legs.

After four doctors, two specialists, and six months, they'd finally received a diagnosis. A pink-lipped, blonde doctor, her voice light and giggling like a young girl's, telling him that he would never dance again, that M.S. would slowly take away everything he had ever known. Ever loved. How Carin had wanted to slap that baby-voiced, Barbie-faced bitch and tell her to talk like an adult instead of a goddamn child. Her palms had itched with the want.

Again, she went to the kitchen window and looked for him in the gloom.

He hadn't turned on any lights. She frowned. He did this sometimes. When he was immersed in a rehearsal or new choreography, he would forget to eat or to sleep. Once, when they'd first been married, he hadn't come home, lost himself in the tying together of music and muscle, and she'd spent the night curled in the bathtub, the water turning cold around her. The next morning he'd hugged her to him, his chest and stomach hard under the dark sweater he wore, and swore that he would love her until his body couldn't remember how to breathe.

Still. He shouldn't be using a saw in the dark, and she moved toward the door that led into their backyard.

She called his name into the black, the wind whipping her words away from her before the winter night swallowed them. Shivering, she stood in the doorway taking her right foot on and off of the top stair. The saw came to life for a brief moment before settling once more into silence.

He's fine. He can take care of himself. He's not a child, she thought, and she turned back, left the door slightly open for him. He would be disappointed if she went to him and spoiled the thing he'd worked on all day. Especially now. As if the disease blooming inside of him had already eaten through what little he had left. As if she didn't trust him to be able to do this thing for her. Something so simple. A thing a husband should be able to do for a wife.

With methodical care she cooked a dinner she wouldn't eat and packed it in the refrigerator in case Benjamin was hungry when he finally came inside. There was a decent bottle of Malbec, and she opened it, didn't bother with a glass.

At midnight, she was drunk. Somewhere beyond the kitchen, Benjamin hammered at the door, and the rhythmic pounding coupled with the wine made her sleepy. Leaning into the couch, she closed her eyes and vanished into the smell of clean wood. Somehow, it had seeped into the house, stealing in through the crack at the bottom of the door. It didn't bother her anymore. Benjamin had been right.

It could have been hours or minutes later when the sound woke her. A light scritching, like something wrapped in heavy fabric dragging itself across the hardwoods. She caught her breath and willed her heart to be silent and listened to the heavy silence of the house. One. Two. Took a breath and let it out. Slowly, slowly. Tried not to think of the fear curling hard and sharp in her belly.

The sound stopped, and she had the distinct feeling of it moving, turning back. Something crawling on its belly from the kitchen toward the back door.

Benjamin must have come inside because all of the lights were off. He would have gone through the rooms and switched them off one by one, moving quietly to avoid waking her. She could picture him stumbling in, tired and aching from a long day of work, and letting the door fall shut behind him without the latch catching properly before going to bed. An animal—a squirrel or a possum —had found its way into the house seeking warmth from the frigid night. This was the sound. Had to be the sound she heard now. She couldn't let herself think of the possibility of anything else.

The sound had turned, was moving away from the kitchen door. The crawling thing making its way out of the kitchen, past the dining táble on the left, and toward the living room where she lay trying not to breathe. Whatever the animal was, it was much larger than she had originally thought. A dog, maybe? But why would it creep around like that, dragging itself along on its belly?

She could hear its breath now, slow and even. Certainly not a squirrel or a possum. Too large for that. Too large even for a dog. Something the size of a man. Benjamin had not closed the door, and now an intruder had slipped between their walls, would open her up with his teeth and use the parts he could. This was what she thought to herself as she listened.

Her heart hammered in the back of her throat, and she squeezed her eyes shut, willed herself to move, to scream, to do anything but keep still. It was a simple thing to sit up, to reach over and switch on the lamp resting on the end table next to the couch, but the thought of the creature on the floor kept her frozen in place.

"Carin?"

Her breath whooshed out, her lungs burning and aching.

"Benjamin?"

"Are you awake?"

"What the fuck? Are you okay? What are you doing?" She sat up quickly, reached a hand for him, but he shrank away from her, tucked himself further into darkness. She squinted but could only make out the outline of his frame prostrate against the floor.

"Come to bed with me."

"Did you fall? Let me help you."

"Didn't fall. Just worn out. Didn't want to wake you. Come to bed with me," he said again. His voice was strange. Tired. Like he used to sound after a long day in the studio.

It didn't explain why he'd been crawling in the dark.

He must have fallen. He would have been ashamed, wouldn't have wanted her to know that it was happening so quickly. The disintegration of this graceful body. His own private hell laid bare.

"Yeah. Of course," she said, stood, and without thinking, reached for him again.

"Carin? Who are you talking to?" The voice, Benjamin's voice, came from directly behind her. Not the form lying before her in the soft dark. Her knees buckled, and she stumbled forward, the room suddenly flooded with light as Benjamin turned on a lamp.

There was nothing there. No strange man huddled in the corner, no terrifying doppleganger of her husband. Only the paisley area rug and a large basket she used for laundry next to the fireplace.

Turning, she looked at her husband. Rumpled t-shirt, his hair tousled from sleep.

"I was dreaming," she said, but even as the words left her mouth she felt the untruth in them. They fell from her tongue like dead things.

"You were talking," he said and smiled.

"Overly tired. I do that sometimes."

He nodded and pulled her to him. His skin smelled of cedar, bright and clean, but as she breathed, the smell turned sour, almost fetid, and she pulled away.

"Come to bed," he said and reached across her to turn off the lamp before moving down the hallway. For several moments, she waited, let her eyes re-adjust to the darkness and listened to the mattress springs creaking beneath Benjamin's weight. She would not look back into that corner. She would not.

When she made her way to their bedroom, Benjamin was already asleep. That night, she locked their bedroom door. Outside, the creature moved up and down the hallway. She did not sleep.

"WHAT?"

"You sick or something?" He reached for her face, brushed her bangs away from her eyes. A gesture he'd made habit while they were dating, but it had been so long since he'd touched her like this. Something light and affectionate not tainted by the darker thing lurking under his skin.

"No. Didn't sleep well," she said, and he nodded, tucked back into the stack of pancakes before him.

"Your appetite."

"Mmm?"

"You haven't been hungry like this. Not for a while."

"I guess so."

She pushed her fork into the cooling stack of pancakes on her own plate, pulled it back and watched as the holes filled with syrup and closed over like blood clotting a wound. When he'd woken that morning, stumbled into the bathroom, she went to the door, thought of whispering through the wood about the sound, that *thing* creeping up and down their hallway, but she swallowed the words, laughed at how stupid she was acting. She was stressed. Hadn't slept well in months. There had been no sound. No second Benjamin.

"I didn't know you could carve," she said.

"Something about the wood. It's hard to explain," he said. She looked at him, but he kept his eyes down, focused on the plate before him. Whatever had come in the night may have been a product of her mind, but she could still hear that soft scraping, could still hear the sound of a body pulling itself up and down the hallway.

"Don't come out, okay? I want it to be a surprise."

The repeated phrase bothered her. She set down her fork.

"I've never seen you carve," she said, and he glanced up at her then. Blue eyes cold and burning, and she immediately regretted intruding on this moment. He wanted to impress her. To show her that he wasn't beaten yet, and here she was doing her best to fuck it all up.

"Of course. I'll be here. Getting drunk. Maybe wandering around naked. You'll be missing a good opportunity."

He grinned at her, his eyes flashing, but then snatched up his hat, kissed her, and whispered in her ear, his breath sweet and cloying.

"There's so much we can't see. Everything that's underneath. Hiding. But it wants us to see, to pull it out from where it's sleeping and make it beautiful again."

He was out the door before she could open her mouth.

HOW LONG HAD she been standing in the hallway? Benjamin's words were still in her ear, swelling and bloating with impossible weight.

"Everything that's underneath," she repeated.

She'd come looking for some evidence, some sign to prove she wasn't crazy. A groove carved into the floor, a hair, anything that justified the reality of the sound she'd heard in the night. Pulling herself onto her belly, she crawled along the floor, her cheek pressed against the wooden boards, fingers probing.

After an hour of doing little more than bruising her ribs from crawling along the floor, she gave up. It was when she turned out the light, in that brief flash, that she saw something. Each time she thought she saw more of the shape, but then she doubted herself. As soon as the light was on, she absolutely believed that it was nothing more than her eyes playing tricks, and so she flipped the switch off again, squinted into the growing dark.

The back door opened and closed, but she did not turn away, did not look back over her shoulder to see her husband creeping through the kitchen, his fingernails digging into the floor. Surely, he would be creeping. All of the things slumbering inside of him coming awake, waiting to be seen, waiting to be found in the dark.

"Come and see, Carin," he said, and she flicked the light once more. On. Off. The shape did not move, but she could make out what looked like teeth. She thought she would laugh, or cry, or scream, but every sound stayed locked in her throat.

"Come and see the door. Come and see what I've found," he said.

"I can't. Please," she said. If she followed him now, the world would come undone. All of the shadows would come to life and grow teeth. Bite and tear until there was nothing left.

"It's so beautiful, love. Come and see."

"Please, Benjamin," she said, but somehow, her legs carried her forward. Her fear, hard and razor sharp, unfolded inside of her.

He waited for her on the back steps, his legs scrabbling across the wood like a spider's, and led her out into the night.

It had begun to snow, but the flakes looked tinged with grey, as if night had stained their surface, and she swiped at her hair, afraid that somehow by simply touching it, the darkness would leak, like poison, into her as well.

She followed him past the row of camellias she had planted, past the vegetable boxes she had put to bed back in October. Her feet were freezing. She had forgotten to put on shoes.

There was no light in the shed, but she could hear him before her, that slow, methodical dragging.

"Benjamin?"

"Can you see it? The whole world opened up. Waiting." His voice was high, breathy with excitement.

It took a moment for her eyes to adjust, to take in the massive cedar door Benjamin had built. He'd suspended it somehow—a series of ropes and pulleys—and it hovered above the ground. Strange wormlike shapes with round mouths and jagged teeth carved into the surface, their bodies tangling together in some kind of obscene orgiastic experience. Here and there a proboscis extended, probing into the chests of what appeared to be human torsos, the hands held up in supplication.

"So beautiful once you open the door and look. Once you *really* look. Like the wood. Waiting to be seen and touched. Then it opens you up, swallows down all of the sin and the hurt and the damage. You can't imagine. What it's like to be whole again."

He stood then, his full height towering over her, his toes cracking as he extended his body into arabesque, laughing as he went en pointe. Something his body should not be able to do.

Behind her, came the sound of something pulling itself on hands and knees through snow.

The door really was beautiful. Deep amber tints that glowed without light. A color she could wrap herself in and forget this past year. All of the struggle and pain and doubt that she'd had in herself and her marriage. Wondering if she was truly strong enough to carry Benjamin—to carry the both of them—through a future that promised only loss.

"Don't you want to open the door, Carin?" Benjamin said, and turned, his pirouette a quick, almost violent movement.

Benjamin's lips did not move, but his voice came from behind her. A voice that belonged to deep earth and snow and dark. A gaping mouth waiting to take everything that had left her bleeding and raw.

"Something good," she whispered.

Benjamin laughed, his body turning impossibly fast, moving into a blurred fouetté. She had forgotten how to breathe. The smell of cedar everywhere.

Then, she laughed, too, and opened the door.

The Wicked Shall Come
Upon Him

Twain met the girl on a night without stars. In the months leading up to her, darkness had bled from the edges of the heavens, blotting out what had once glowed with quiet, white light.

Before the sky had swallowed itself, the moon had bloated, heavy and full. Later, it turned a rancid yellow, and people closed their doors and curtains to avoid the moonlight.

It took two weeks for the moon to leak into people's skins, turning it the color of something spoiled, rotted. An effect of the environment, the news said, and night after night, people drowned themselves with pills and booze in the hopes that they could ignore the screams pouring from the blackened sky.

People talked in low voices to each other, to themselves. Tried to dismiss their yellowing skins as a temporary effect of the moon's shift, to brush off the screams as a seismic event. Every day another set of scientists on the television explained that eventually the moon would resume its natural pattern, but each morning, nothing had changed. The sun rose and shone without warmth. The night kept coming, and shadow spread like a blanket over the world.

Outside, under the darkness, people set fire to what they

could find. Tore apart furniture. Couches and dining tables piled in front of their homes and set aflame. The darkness held at bay with weak, flickering light.

They fucked and sweated and pissed in the dirt. Hunted needles and injected confusion and chaos into their veins. A never-ending orgy at the end of the world.

Like rats, they found themselves outside, seeking the light of the many fires. This is where Twain saw the girl. Outside of the apartment building in the courtyard he came to sometimes smoke, her lanky body crouched before a tree, long dark hair twisted into dreadlocks tipped with blue. He watched her peel apples with a razor blade. Long strips fluttered and twisted underneath her hands as the edge bit against white flesh.

"You one of Nathan's?" the girl asked him.

He didn't like the easy nature of Nathan's name in her mouth. Didn't like the way she assumed that he was just another fuck. *One of Nathan's.* The tone of her voice implying that he was nothing. He stroked the platinum band on his left hand, his fingers tracing the metal that covered the date inscribed beneath.

"We were married. Once. Before," he said.

She nodded. "And now?"

"He wanted to throw a party. Outside. For the last time. Before whatever the fuck's going to happen happens," he said.

The words were husks, dead shells of what he wanted to speak. He'd learned to swallow the sharp teeth of his love, and the silence he carried within him was the only thing that kept him from grasping the girl's razor and drawing it across his throat.

"How do you know Nathan?"

"He's easy to know. Everyone knows him," she said.

She was right. It was why he had fallen in love with Nathan when he was nothing more than a child. A seventeen-year-old high school dropout in the big city. He'd haunted the bars, giving the bouncers blowjobs in trash-filled back alleys to get in.

The knees of his jeans absorbing liquid runoff from the garbage bins and rats bumping against his shoes as he stared into the distance, tried not to focus on the sweating, heaving muscle in front of him.

He'd met Nathan at Mary's on karaoke night, had watched him onstage growling out Tom Waits to a crowd screaming for him to take his fucking shirt off already.

Four bourbon waters later, he approached Nathan, screamed over the pumping music that Tom Waits sucked ass. To which Nathan laughed, called him a baby, and bought him another drink.

When the bar closed, Nathan pushed him into a cab, and they clawed at one another the entire twenty minutes to Nathan's apartment. In the living room, Twain learned the movements of Nathan's body, the taste of his sweat. He held it under his tongue, marveled at how love can blossom, hard and violent, like thorns shooting into the heart. Later, they spooned, Nathan's pale skin standing in stark contrast with Twain's dark, and Nathan had teased him. Sang "Ebony and Ivory" as he wrapped himself around Twain.

Nathan had a way of speaking that made you lean into him, like he was telling you a secret. Like you were the only two people in the world. Twain had leaned into him as they whispered to each other. He'd wished that he could burrow inside Nathan's chest and plant himself so deep he would never be torn out and tossed away. They drowsed until morning light streaked through the windows over Nathan's bed.

Twain fell in love with him that first night. Three weeks later, they stood before a Justice of the Peace, and Nathan swore to love him until their bodies crumbled into dust.

"I'm Cass," the girl said, and Twain started. He had forgotten her presence there, and she smiled up at him, her lips pressed in a tight line.

He opened his mouth to speak, but a quick movement to the left drew his attention. Two nude forms tumbled out of the dark, their skins sallow and streaked in dirt. Nathan and a man he didn't recognize, their arms draped over each other, the man whispering into Nathan's ear. His breath would be hot, thick with whisky or wine, and Nathan would suck the words from his lips as if he were drawing the very essence out of him.

He swallowed. Watched the sky for something other than darkness, but there was nothing to see. Above them, the screams sounded again, a discordant melody of pain or hunger. Twain was afraid to know which.

When it had all began, Nathan disappeared for hours at a time. Came home reeking of smoke and liquor. On the night the moon vanished, Nathan had told him, "Why not have a good time while we can? Fuck who we want. Do what we want. Everything's going to shit, Twain. Can't we just *live*? For once in our lives, let's just forget the rules and do what we want."

"Fuck you, Nathan. If you bring anyone in here, into our *home*, I swear to Christ I'll fucking kill him," he'd said. He'd wanted to hit him. Wanted to feel Nathan's blood under his fingernails and to know that it belonged to *him*. This blood was his alone, and he would tear apart anything that tried to take it from him. He would die before that happened.

The next week, their sheets breathed another man's smell. All of the anger, all of the rage he'd felt the moment Nathan had told him what he planned to do melted away into a sobbing desperation.

He locked himself in the bathroom and swallowed the first bottle of pills he could find. Aspirin, it turned out. He thought his stomach had turned inside out, and he'd shit his pants, but his heart kept pounding in his chest. Nathan had not been there to hold it in.

Despite everything, he couldn't bring himself to leave.

"If I carve your name, carve The Sign, into one of these, you'll fall in love with me." Cass twitched the razor toward the apples under her boots, and grinned. Her teeth were stained red.

"Wine?"

"What's that?"

"Red wine. Bitch of a stain."

"Should I do it? Should I cut your life into mine, Twain? Make you forget him? Forget the sound of your name in his mouth; the weight of his hand against your chest? All of your learned routines. Gone. Poof. Like smoke. You would be happy again."

Somewhere in the dark, Nathan laughed. He could no longer tell the sound from the screaming.

"How much more? How much more do I have to feel before there's nothing left?" he asked Cass. She shrugged her shoulders.

There was too much space in this new world the darkness had created. The fire casting a scant glow, and all of the shadowed things that lived beyond the haloed light stretching toward them, mouths gaping and hungry. Too many empty places where silence echoed through the words Nathan spoke.

Every day, other people drew their yellowed skins around them, cocooning the soft, fragile bits. All so they wouldn't see, wouldn't expose their raw, bleeding hearts. So they could ignore the empty sky and the possibility of whatever came next.

He could have done the same. He had tried. But Nathan would touch him, would tousle his hair, and he found himself confused and suffocating in what had been their love.

Cass picked up another apple, traced the blade over the surface, her fingers appearing to shimmer. The blue fire of stars under her fingernails. He blinked, and the light vanished. She dipped into the apple. Began to carve.

"Why do you think it screams? The sky?" she said.

"I don't know."

"The sign. The Tattered King. He pours his dark over the world. Prepares us for his return from death. And it will *all* fall upon us. All of it."

Her words woke something inside of him, and his stomach

twisted into knots. Strange to be frightened of the words spoken by a girl he didn't even know, but the fear grew all the same.

"Twain! Come the fuck on already. Everybody's waiting." Nathan's voice seeming to come from everywhere at once. He thought the sound would tear him open. He couldn't breathe. The sky bore down, the screams pitching ever higher.

"Everything devours itself. Lust. Hate. Love. We burn and burn until there is only ash, and then we eat what remains. Carry it inside of us like a secret. Until it grows into something else." She brought an apple to her lips, bit down. Red teeth. White flesh.

He shuddered. Turned in the direction of Nathan's voice. He would take one of Nathan's pills. Chase it with whisky or vodka or absinthe. Forget the girl and the sky and her strange mentions of signs and dead kings. Forget the cold fear that had crawled up his spine when Cass spoke. Forget Nathan sweating and grunting against someone else. Forget the way Nathan had looked at him the day they met.

"So easy to do. To slip your fingers under the skin of love. Tug until it drops away. Show everything that lives underneath. All the broken little things," Cass said and took up another apple. Her wrist flicked. A small movement, and he felt himself tipping forward. An abyss yawning before him.

"The King has sent his sign. He will satisfy all of us. Give us what we need. Make us forget. Aren't you hungry, Twain?"

To forget. To have never known Nathan. To have his memory erased. To forget the pain of Nathan laughing, his head leaned against another man's chest. Forget.

"What happens if I say yes?" he asked her, and she stood— she was taller than he'd imagined—and pressed her lips to his. Her tongue was sweet, and he gagged.

Still, he opened his mouth wider to accept what she gave him. He closed his eyes, and dark stars blazed behind his lids. The moon glowed crimson. She poured the sky's screams into him, and they burned. Burned away everything. Bright and clean.

He didn't know when the girl pulled away, only that she had gone, the apples piled beneath his feet, her taste still in his mouth. The fire that Nathan had started had gone out, and the darkness licked at him. Filled him to the brim. He took off his shirt, his pants.

"Twain! What the fuck are you doing out there?" Nathan called, his voice floating from the entrance to the apartment building at his back.

He shouldn't still know that this was Nathan's voice, should he? Shouldn't feel the sudden need to move toward the sound, his feet finding their way back, his heart quickening. She had promised. This supposed King had *promised*.

They lived on the ground floor of an apartment building that had been mostly abandoned. Vast rooms that carried only the ghosts of those who had once lived there. Family portraits still hanging in entryways; a pair of green rain boots left outside the door of 1406; an empty crib pushed against a bare window, a ragged stuffed elephant still inside.

He'd seen people packing, seen them loading cars with boxes, trash bags stuffed with clothing, but he could not remember their faces. These people who shared his walls nothing more than a wisp of memory.

Those who remained drifted in and out. Vague, amorphous shapes that he avoided when he encountered them in the lobby or the hallways, head down, eyes averted. If the others did the same, he didn't know.

He walked into the apartment now, found Nathan in the center of five men. All blonde. Smooth. Hairless. So much the opposite of Twain with his dark skin and dark eyes and thick hair that covered his arms and chest. So much the thing Nathan never claimed to want.

The entryway, lined with cheap Fuseli prints, opened to the living room, the tiny kitchen to the right. The refrigerator stood open, and bottles lined the countertop where a lone candle sputtered and cast shadowed devils against the ceiling. The air was stale and laced with the acrid smell of something faintly chemical.

The fake leather couch and Ikea end tables had been pushed against the walls of the living room to create open floor space. Nathan had taken their sheets and pillows, draped and piled them into some kind of obscene fort where these men he did not know wrapped muscled arms around each other.

Nested in a mound of blankets, Nathan reached for him. His pupils were too large, a deep black threatening to drown the sclera. He didn't want to see him like this. The other men reached for him, too. A knotted tangle of limbs and fingers grasping at his naked legs, his bare belly.

"I've been waiting forever," Nathan said. *Forever.* The word hit him with the force of a bullet.

"I can't. We can't," he said, but Nathan tossed his hair, laughed. Twain's head swam, and the candle flame jumped, divided into two, then four, then hundreds of candles burning.

From the corner of the room, Cass came crawling, her mouth drawn away from her teeth. The gums had gone black, and Twain's gorge rose in the back of his throat at the sight. He swallowed. Took a deep breath.

"Nathan. Please," he said, and the girl wrapped herself around his legs, her fingers burning against his calf.

"Jesus, Twain. Lighten up. Always so fucking intense. Have a drink. Or, if you're feeling frisky, Tyler here has something that will blow your goddamn mind."

"Please," he whispered, but Nathan drew him down among them. Mouths seeking the soft, exposed parts of him and the taste of apples on his tongue as he pushed them away.

Inside of him, the darkness moved, and he pictured tearing out the throats of the men with his bare hands, their yellowed skin withering beneath his touch. He would use their blood as a canvas; draw the King's sign with his finger.

If Cass was still there, he could not find her among the mass of moving flesh.

Flashes of light blinded him. Nathan laughing. Nathan sleeping, his hands tucked beneath him like a child. Nathan holding him as he sobbed on the day his mother died.

He wondered if what the girl had given him would leak out of him, dribble from his lips like poison. If it was even possible for his bones to hold so much darkness. A pain so much like love. Everything and nothing all at once.

When he opened his mouth, the sky resumed its screaming. Whatever lived there, whatever dark angel or King or god, shrieked, and the darkness stole into the room. The entryway, the bottles, the kitchen, fading into a blackened nothing. The men shrieked and clutched at one another, scrambled backward, but there was nowhere to go.

One by one, the other men were swallowed in shadow until only Twain and Nathan remained. And Cass. She crouched beside them, her tongue darting over her lips.

Wherever the others had gone, Twain hoped their skins would be peeled from muscle, their tongues torn from their mouths. Hoped their blood would feed the sky, pour into the moon's ancient craters and carve strange sanguine rivers on the surface. And the King would drink and be satisfied.

"Twain. Oh, God. Oh, *God*. It's happening, isn't it? It's fucking happening. Oh, Jesus."

"What's left now, Nathan? Here at the end. What's left?"

"Jesus. Oh, Jesus. Fuck." Nathan's eyes were wild, beads of sweat appearing on his upper lip, his forehead.

"Why wasn't it enough? Why wasn't *I* enough? We could have gone into the dark together. One body. One flesh."

He could smell Nathan's fear, could feel the rapid beating of his heart quivering in the air. How much he wanted to take that delicate beating in his palm, cup it inside his hands to keep it safe.

"I've carried you inside of me. No matter how I try to starve you out, forget that you were ever there, you won't *leave*. I never wanted anything else, Nathan. There was never anything else."

The darkness hovered over them, waiting. The black just barely touching their legs, reaching for its brother that had curled inside of Twain. Soon, it would cover everything. They would never leave this place.

Still, the darkness drew nearer to them, covered their lower bodies like a mantle.

"I can't feel my feet, Twain. What the fuck? I can't feel anything."

"She gave it to me. The sign. It should be so much easier now. You're still inside of me. Still burning," he said. He wanted to cry, but there were no tears left.

Nathan wrapped his arms around him, and Twain leaned into the man he loved, breathed in the smell of his skin, the feeling of his hands against his neck.

Around them, the sky gaped open, the darkness enveloping everything. The King returning to a world that had forgotten him, left him behind.

"I understand," he whispered to the dark, to the abandoned King. He pressed his mouth to Nathan's, breathed into him. One flesh. One heart.

Together, they waited.

To Sleep Long, to Sleep Deep

Simon had been gone for three days before the phone call came through. After, there had been the identification of the pieces of his body found in the woods, the immeasurable hours of questions in cold rooms with bitter coffee and a fat slug of a detective who eyed Nina's cleavage like it was a piece of chicken he very much wanted to sink his teeth into.

"And you don't know where he went after he left the residence?" the detective said, wiping a line of sweat from his upper lip.

"No. We fucked. He left. End of story," she said, delighting in the sudden flush streaking up his neck, a sick red creeping against doughy flesh.

Even though they held her in that room for three days, nothing they had stuck, so they released her into a bright October morning that was uncharacteristically warm. She walked home along Hwy. 92, her legs unshaven but exposed in a too tight skirt, and ignored the honks from horny truckers or pissed off business women when she stumbled too far over the white line.

She liked the daring of it, the sharp wind as the cars went

whooshing by. For a moment, it was almost like the first time, when Simon had found the book and brought it to her. Almost like the first time she'd read the words, and the thing that lived there had fought its way out and curled inside of her, slithered behind her eyes and spoken in a voice like jagged glass. It had hurt at first, but eventually, she could read the words without pain knifing through her belly, and at the end, before Simon took the book away, there had been heat between her legs, a low throbbing threatening to spill.

Simon had been jealous. Angry that the thing in the book had picked her instead of him. After all, he'd been the one to find it, the cracked leather binding hidden among cheap paperbacks at a used bookstore he'd happened upon in New York. No author listed, no title on the front cover. He'd told her that the salesman hadn't recognized it but sold it any way when Simon offered him fifty on the spot.

He'd bought it for the illustrations. Full page, sepia-toned depictions of vivisections, bodies peeled open like ripe fruits while grinning devils lapped up spilled blood, or flies and maggots eating away at piles of intestines, the darkly gleaming insects so perfectly rendered Nina thought she could see them squirming. Once, when Simon had left her with the book, she touched each page to be sure, but there had only been ink. He spent hours with it, turning the pages slowly, trailing his fingers over the pictures, his mouth slack as saliva dripped from his chin.

His obsession with the macabre had never bothered her. She figured it was one of the few things he liked about her—the fact that she didn't spew when he dragged her to splatter porn films or didn't run screaming from the room when he told her that he'd always fantasized about doing it with a corpse. She'd learned that when it came to keeping her bed warm, it was better to go numb.

And then the thing in the book had spoken to her. It squirmed somewhere along her spine, like a spider twitching to life after a long, long winter, and suddenly she could read the nonsensical symbols. As she read, the markings and her thoughts tumbling against each other, the thing whispered, "Aren't you tired, Nina?" and something in her came loose.

She could never remember what was written on the pages. After she closed the book, her mind was dull, fogged, and she spent long hours trying to recall the words only to have them slip through her fingers. There was only the voice saying over and over "Aren't you tired?"

She was tired. Tired of Simon stumbling into the darkness of the bedroom, the sharp tang of whiskey on his breath as he bit her lower lip. Always too hard. Always too rough. He liked to bite, to twist her arms behind her back until she whimpered against him, his taste in her mouth. Like salt. Like earth.

"Aren't you tired?" the voice had said to her as Simon stared at the illustrations, his face bone pale, a slick of sweat shining on his forehead as he fought against a scream. He didn't care about the words, only the terrible pictures, and she would look away when he came in his pants, his face contorted, his teeth bared.

She started to hate him. Wished he would go away and leave her alone with the book. He couldn't even read it, didn't know what it felt like for the thing to slip into his body, for the voice to speak to him. It could change her. It had promised. Change her so that she would never be tired again. Make her something new. Something strong.

When Simon slept, Nina would open the book and read until gray morning seeped through the windows. Her hair began to fall out in clumps. The skin on her back and shoulders grew rough and chapped, her fingers lengthening, the knuckles crooking upward.

When the book disappeared, Simon had told her she was obsessed, couldn't control herself, and so he had sold it. But every afternoon Simon would leave the house for hours. "Running errands," he'd said. After that, the voice went quiet, and two weeks later, Simon was found ripped to shreds in the woods, his body dripping into the spongy moss under a circlet of fir trees.

The blood did not appear until five days after the police sent her home. It came, painting the kitchen window in crimson gore, and she knew it was Simon. Day after day, she watched the window, waited for him to haunt her, but for weeks there was only the blood.

Then she heard him. His step always in the next room or just behind her, his breath hitching beside her as she slept, but when she turned, the sound evaporated, and there was a fluttering of pain behind her eyes in the place where the thing had once whispered.

Weeks passed, and the wash of blood slowed, faded from a deep, viscous smear to Valentine's candy pink. Simon's pillow was still cold despite the small curl of auburn hair placed just so against the thin cotton. *A talisman*, she thought, but not even the hair that she'd found after scouring their bedroom floor worked. She'd tried it all. A torn Ramones T-shirt thrown across her bed. His vinyl collection pulled out of the sleeves and scattered on the floor. The sluttish nightie he'd bought during their trip to Denver tossed in the corner as if in a hurried state of undress.

None of it worked. It didn't matter that she hadn't really loved him, that he had only seen her as pretty skin covering an empty, skittering collection of thought and emotion. "If you could just shut the fuck up for five seconds, you'd be perfect," he'd told her, and she knew she'd become a statistic—the woman trapped in an emotionally abusive relationship, but she'd let him move in with her. Because he'd brought her the book.

Night bled into day. Her head began to ache. She couldn't sleep. Could only sit by the window and watch.

"Where's the book, Simon?" she shouted, but there was no response, only the silence of the house mocking her. He could not take it away. The book had spoken to her, had chosen her, but the harder she tried to draw him out, the rituals growing more involved and complex, the more he withdrew, until the window was wet only with rain, and the empty spaces inside her roared.

"Where's the goddamn book?" she repeated over and over, a litany offered to a ghost. In the night, she sometimes heard him, the small noises he'd once made beside her, but when she held her breath, strained her ears against the quiet, she heard only the pulsing of her own heartbeat.

The night that she walked into the woods for the second time, it snowed.

"Here. Right here." She drew a small circle with the toe of her boot.

"You fucker," she hissed and pushed her fingers through the crust of snow to the dirt beneath, brought it to her lips. The grit lodged in her teeth. "I can still taste you. Your *stench*." She spat, then shoveled more dirt in.

"Is this what you want? You want me here? Like I'm supposed to be sorry? You took it away, Simon. It wanted *me*."

The fat detective had told her about the bite marks on Simon's body, but they had been so jagged, so torn, they could not be identified as human or animal. They'd swabbed the skin for saliva, hoping for DNA, but the results had been inconclusive, pointed toward a strange hybrid of spider venom, dog saliva, and traces of semen.

From the cold spaces hidden in the forest, came a guttural, animalistic screaming that, for a moment, she thought was Simon finally materializing before her, but there was the taste of blood in her throat, and she realized that the sounds came from her. She grunted, pushed her face into the snow, rooted past the rotting leaves, dragged her tongue along the ground, tasting, searching for the book.

She'd followed him here that last night. Crawled on all fours, scrabbled beneath the brush so he would not see. Her eyes able to see in the dark, she'd watched him bury something, and there was the slightest stirring between her legs, the thing coming awake before slipping back into the black. The book. He had the book.

Even after Simon was dead, the exposed bones licked clean, she had not been able to find the book, had dug hole after hole until her fingernails peeled backward. *Ashes to ashes*, she had thought and cackled before pushing her face into the dirt, raked her hands back and forth, back and forth.

"Where is it?" she shrieked and clawed at her eyes, gathered fistfuls of hair and scattered the loose strands into the wind.

He was teasing her. She knew it. She could have been one of those haunted women, the kind they put on TV, pouring their grief into cameras and microphones as D-rate actors played out the romance of their hauntings. But in death, as in life, Simon wasn't the romantic type. He wanted her to know he was there, that he would never show her where he'd left the book.

She writhed on the ground, her skin bloodied and chapped, the snow turning pink. She could not bear it.

Once more, she began to dig. When the flesh ripped away from her fingertips, she used her teeth, tore at the frozen earth. Slowly, the ground opened around her, swallowed her up as she went deeper, pushing mouthfuls of dirt past her gullet, gagging then swallowing.

Down there, in the bowels of the world, the voice waited for her. She licked her lips, tasted Simon in the grit and the sand and the roots. He could haunt her forever, but it didn't matter.

She would have the book, and when she found it, the voice would fill her up, and she would rest. But first there was only the digging, only the taste of blood in her mouth as she pushed further on, further down.

The Fleshtival

"The Fleshtival," Paul said, dark eyes shining from behind a smear of black hair that he hadn't washed in four days. The city had cut water to his apartment on Monday, and fucking Vinnie wouldn't have cash for him until tonight.

"Where the hell do you hear about shit like this," Jake said, exhaled a mouthful of grey smoke, and handed the joint back to Paul.

Paul grinned, a mouth full of too white, too straight teeth. His dad was a dentist, and if Paul had nothing else, he had teeth like a fucking celebrity. "Somebody taped a flyer to my door." He paused, reached onto the coffee table, and pulled the crumpled piece of paper from beneath a collection of beer bottles with the labels peeled off. A nervous habit Paul had never been able to shake. "A thousand bucks, and they roll out the red carpet. Read that shit, man. 'Pussy for *miles.*' I mean, they don't call it the fucking Fleshtival for nothing."

Paul took another pull from the joint, and held the acrid smoke inside of his lungs until he coughed, his stomach clenching around nothing. When was the last time he had eaten? He'd spent his last roll of cash on the baggie that lay empty before them and a bottle of pills that Nathan said was Molly, but Paul thought was actually just a bunch of muscle relaxers his dealer had filched from his grandmother's medicine cabinet. Well, fuck that guy. He'd taken four of the pills the night before, and fell into darkness unlike anything he remembered. If nothing else, those little pills gave him a one-way ticket to Dreamland and with the shit sleep he'd been getting lately, Paul would take what he could get.

"No way that this is real. This has hoax written all over it," Jake said.

"Well, I'm going. Can't win if you don't play, right? I mean Jesus Christ, dude. Anything you want them to do, they'll do it. Girl after girl after girl. Any fucked up little thing, they smile and ask if you want more than one of them to do it to you. At once. Says so on the flyer." Paul waved the piece of paper at Jake's stupid mug. "Can you believe it? And what's the likelihood of something like this happening again ever in your fucking life, man? Twenty-two years old and still a virgin, and a goddamn *fleshtival* comes along, and you're pussing out?" Paul squinted at Jake, reached out a finger and poked at the soft rolls of fat pouring over a pair of khaki shorts.

"Cut it the fuck out, Paul," Jake said and swatted his hand away.

Grinning, Paul slapped him. Not hard. Just enough to let Jake know that he was only fucking around.

"Bitch tits. Don't be a little bitch tits, Jake."

"I fucking hate it when you call me that."

"So don't be a bitch tits then, you little fucker."

Jake sighed. A deep, heavy sigh that let Paul know that he was giving in, and Paul gripped the joint between his teeth and smiled.

"So what happens when we get out there and this thing doesn't exist?"

Paul took another hit, let the smoke fill him up. "I dunno, man. If it's not real, you keep your money, drive back, and spend your Saturday night whacking it to old episodes of *Law and Order*. No harm, no foul."

"You really are a piece of shit, you know?" Jake said.

Paul thumped him on the back. "'Atta' boy. Knew you'd come through."

Paul had considered it a fortuitous day when Jake answered his Craigslist ad. He'd needed a new roommate after his last one had beaten the shit out of him and stolen three hundred dollars and a bag of his best weed. If he ever saw that fucker on the street, Paul intended to pound the shit out of his balls until the guy coughed blood and begged for mercy. That would teach him to fuck around with Paul Campbell.

Leaning back, Paul stared at the ceiling. The Tool poster he bought when he was sixteen hung over him, and he raised a finger, pointed dead in the center of Maynard James Keenan's forehead, and mouthed a silent "pow" that seemed to detonate in the center of Paul's brain. Everything seeming to dribble away in a white-hot stream of fluid. Nathan may be a piece of shit when it came to pills, but he knew his fucking weed. If anything, he could thank his two-bit dealer for a decent high and a good night's sleep.

"It's only supposed to be here for one night. Up in New Hope. Some secret place in the woods. You're supposed to find a sign with a red ribbon and park there and then just walk into the trees. They find you, and then it's fucking heaven until the sun comes up."

"Tonight?"

"Yes, tonight."

"I have to work tonight."

Paul sat back up and looked at his roommate. "Get out of it, dude. Seriously. This is not something to miss out on. Once in a lifetime kind of shit. You know? Get Gary to cover you. He's always whining after your shifts."

"Yeah," Jake said, and Paul leaned forward until Jake's breath streamed warm and sour over his face and stared without blinking into those idiot blue eyes that flinched and darted just over Paul's shoulder.

"Don't you do it, Jake. Don't be a pussy," he said, and Jake nodded, his chins jiggling, and Paul pushed himself away, let the joint burn against his fingers.

"Call Gary. Do it. We're leaving at nine. And clean yourself up. You fucking stink like something died inside of your asshole and crawled into your shorts."

"Fuck you, Paul," Jake said and stood, shuffled off to the bathroom where Paul knew he would douse himself in Axe body spray and cover his ball sack in Gold Bond powder.

Whatever. He didn't really care as long as Jake coughed up his part of the cash. Once they actually got up to New Hope, he was planning on ditching that fat little turd anyway. The very last thing he wanted to see once he finally slid into some hot little piece was Jake's fat ass.

Again, his stomach contracted, and he pushed his palm against it. If he pressed hard enough, it almost felt better, but there was still a lingering flavor in the back of his mouth. Like he'd deep throated a battery. Acidic and burning.

Once Vinnie got here with his cash, he would hit up the burrito joint on 37th, put something inside of him before he put himself inside one of those hot little cherries. Real virgins, the flyer had said. They had real, honest-to-God virgins.

He hadn't had a piece like that since high school. Ronnie and those fucking tits, man. Too big for a girl who wasn't even eighteen yet. She'd told him about the offers she got from the clubs she sneaked into on the weekends. Clubs with sticky floors and watered down drinks and stupid names like Secrets or Twolips.

It was only a matter of time before she started dancing on stage for money instead of on the floor for free, and he'd stopped seeing Ronnie after he had gone to visit her—a surprise—and seen her slobbering all over some guy's dick.

Of course, Ronnie had told him that it was for money, but

he couldn't get the thought of her mouth filled with old dude jizz out his head, and Paul called it off then and there.

Last he heard, Ronnie's tits had started to sag, and the club had downgraded her to Wednesday and Thursday nights. He thought he remembered hearing that she'd had a kid, too. Good thing he got out of there before shit got serious. He needed a kid like he needed a fucking hole in the head.

Closing his eyes, he drifted through the high. Visions of flesh laid bare. Round, smooth curves wrapped around his hips. He hoped that the flyer was real. A thousand bucks wasn't the easiest for him to come by, and if it was just some shitty joke to send him into the woods chasing some mythical pussy circus, heads would roll.

"When's Vinnie supposed to be here?" Jake opened the bathroom door, and the cloying smell of sweat mixed with cheap body spray flooded the room. Paul grimaced.

"Christ, dude. Shut the fucking door. You smell like a turd wrapped inside of a horny seventh grader."

"Sorry," Jake said and flushed crimson. He stepped out of the small bathroom, shutting the door behind him. "Seriously though. I don't want to be here when Vinnie is. Dude gives me the creeps."

"Vinnie's an okay guy."

"The last time he was here, he saw a picture of my little sister on my phone. Said he would do anything to get inside of something like that. She's fucking twelve, Paul. Twelve. I don't want to be here, okay?"

"Okay, okay. He said he would be here at seven. Feel free to disappear."

Jake shuffled back to one of the two small bedrooms at the back of the apartment and closed the door behind him. A few minutes passed before a thumping bass line kicked on. Some shitty rap group that Jake wouldn't shut up about, and Paul quelled the urge to kick down the door and smash his roommate's CD player into tiny bits of plastic.

Two hours. Two hours until Vinnie showed up with his money. Two more hours until he could get the fuck out of this place with its shit brown walls and ratty carpet and dishes piled in the sink and buzzing with flies, their wings a transparent blue hallucination that made him wonder if he was actually seeing them, or only hearing them.

Closing his eyes, he willed himself to sleep, but his mind would not settle, and he snapped his eyes open, looked again at the dark stain that had appeared on the carpet by the entrance to the kitchen two days ago. The size of his fist, it was the deep color of rust, of something gone rancid, and he'd asked Jake about it, who denied that he had spilled anything.

Paul wasn't sure why he believed his roommate, but he let the issue drop, and since then, the spot had grown larger. At least, he thought that it had. It was hard to tell. If it had grown, it was an imperceptible creeping outward, and he had no way to prove that it was getting bigger. Fucking Nina. She'd always been a shit landlord, and now this place was going to hell, and she didn't care. He was probably being eaten alive with some kind of mold, spores twitching through his lungs as he breathed in whatever the fuck grew inside of that dark stain, and she laughed it up down there in her office that she'd had completely renovated last year. That bitch.

When the front door opened, he started, jerking upward, and he winced as his stomach muscles cramped.

"Wakey, wakey, you little shit!"

Vinnie. Early.

Confused, Paul pulled himself up, blinked toward the doorway at the scrawny black guy filling the space.

"You're early."

"Nah, man. Right on time." Vinnie jerked his head toward the digital clock hanging on the wall.

"You alright? Look like you've seen a ghost, brother," Vinnie said, and Paul ground his fists against his eyes, watched strange, bloated colors float behind his eyelids.

He must have fallen asleep. The last he remembered, he was tracing the outlines of the stain. Around and around and around, and then Vinnie's voice had cut through the reverie and scared the ever loving shit out of him.

"Yeah. Fine. Just fell asleep is all," he said, and Vinnie nodded, his locks bouncing against his shoulders.

"Listen. Was only able to get you fifteen hundred. Nobody's in the market for mushrooms any more, dude. Xanax. Ritalin. Heroin. That's what the people want. Nobody wants something a cow shit on."

"Cows don't shit on them."

"Shit on them. Grow in shit. Who cares, man? Thing is no one wants it, so unless you come up with something better, you're cash flow is seriously compromised."

Vinnie flipped a crumpled brown paper bag at him, and Paul thumbed through the bills inside. He could come up with a plan later. For now, he had what he needed for tonight. He licked his lips and counted again. Fifteen hundred. Enough to get him what he wanted and then some.

"Sure. Sure," he said, and Vinnie glanced at him but asked no questions and saw himself to the door.

"For real though, man. You need something new. Something different."

"I heard you. Next week, okay?" Right now, Paul wanted nothing more than for Vinnie to crawl back to whatever shit pit he pulled himself out of and leave him alone. Later, he would come up with another plan, but right now, he needed to take a shower, maybe whack off at least once so that he wouldn't come the second one of the girls wrapped her hands around his cock.

Vinnie tossed a look back before he shouldered through the door, late afternoon sunlight spilling across the frame, and then he was gone as quickly as he had come. Again, Paul rubbed at his eyes, tried to orient himself, but everything felt like it had shifted ten degrees down. He stumbled when he pulled himself to his feet, pitched forward onto the carpet that reeked of cat urine and vomit.

Shaking, he stood. Took a few deep breaths. "Jake?" he called out, but then he remembered that Jake would have left long before Vinnie showed up, and he stumbled into the bathroom, stripped off his Smashing Pumpkins T-shirt and jeans as he turned on the tap.

The showerhead fizzled, but no water fell. *Shit.* He had forgotten that the city had cut the water. He thought he had some Clorox wipes stashed somewhere in the bathroom, and if nothing else, he'd use one of them to scrub his taint and asshole. His pits, too. He wanted to smell nice for the ladies.

Pulling the container from the bottom cabinet, he began the slow process of cleaning himself off. His head still spun, and his tongue—raw and thick in his mouth—felt like it had been run through a meat grinder.

The weed had to have been laced with something. Probably PCP. No way he had just dropped out like that, and his face felt swollen and bruised. Like he'd been in a fight he couldn't win, only he couldn't remember his assailant.

He heard the door open and close again, and he called out. "Jake? That you, man?"

"Yeah."

Paul watched his reflection in the mirror, ran the wipe over his face, and winked. He'd feel better with a hot meal in his belly, and even still, he would rally. Had to. No way was he going to let this moment slip through his fingers because he'd gotten ahold of some laced weed. Fuck that noise.

Tossing the wipe, he stepped out of the bathroom and cracked his knuckles. "Let's roll."

Jake was pale and sweaty. Paul pitied the poor girl that would end up at the raw end of that heaving bag of meat, but Jake nodded and followed Paul out the door into a day that smelled of burnt tar and hot death laid flat on asphalt.

"I KNOW how to get to New Hope."

"Listen. I didn't ask you if you knew how to get to New Hope. I'm telling you where to fucking turn, so just do it and stop complaining."

Night had fallen while Jake drove, and Paul observed the landscape through the windows. Watched trees morph and change into something strange and monstrous, long branches reaching longer fingers into a dark sky without stars.

They hadn't passed another car in at least twenty minutes, and the road had narrowed at some point, the right shoulder dropping off into a deep culvert.

"Here. Red ribbon on the sign." Paul said. "Take a left here."

The car lurched as it turned off of the main road and onto grass. Paul popped open his door before the car came to a full stop, his seatbelt already off, and he jumped out of the car, bracing himself for the inevitable impact.

Walk into the woods. That was it. The girls will find you. Just keep walking. Don't look for them. Don't listen for them. Lose yourself in the trees, in the dark. That was what the flyer had said, and he took off for the tree line, let his gaze fade into the distance. Ignored the sound of the car door slamming as Jake exited. Ignored Jake calling to him, his fat ass scrambling to catch up.

Crashing through the underbrush, Paul dismissed the thorns tearing at his calves, the blood beading before trickling in small lines toward his ankles. When the girls found him, maybe he would get them to lick the blood off of him, watch their tongues dance against his skin before tangling together. He pressed his fist hard against his stomach and kept walking.

Behind Paul, Jake called his name again, but Paul was already too far ahead, and the sound floated into the gloom around him, the mist eating the words, and he hurried onward, his heart thudding hard in his chest.

Paul's stomach twisted, and he swallowed, his Adam's apple working to hold back the acid at the top of his throat. He'd thought that eating something was a good idea, but now, deep among the trees, everything he'd eaten threatened to come back up, and he paused, leaned against a tree and waited for the stream of vomit that would surely come, but he heaved and nothing happened, so he kept walking, leaves slapping at his face.

In and out, he drifted, dreamlike and unhurried, the tree line blurring until all he could see was darkness; the sound of his broken breathing heavy in his ears. In and out. One foot in front of the other, and he tumbled into the black, his legs breaking through underbrush that he could no longer see. No longer feel.

He'd folded the wad of bills Vinnie had given him and put them in his pocket, and they weighed heavily against his leg, a definitive reminder of what he was here for. A chorus singing that he should not give in to that soft darkness. A hymn telling him not to forget, and on he walked.

For minutes or for hours he continued, until there came the touch, feather light, against his shoulder, and he turned to see blonde, rippling curls, a soft, crimson smile, and bare shoulders that seemed to shimmer in the moonlight. Across the girl's cheek, a birthmark the color of rust bloomed. A stain against her otherwise perfect face. Oh well. He could always turn her around when he fucked her.

The girl's hand was hot, and she pressed it over his lips, slipped her fingers down and down and down, until they dipped inside of his right pocket. She pulled the stack of bills into her palm and closed her fist around them.

"We knew that you would come. We've all been waiting. Follow me," she said and turned, led him further into the mass of thin pine trees, the needles slippery and shifting under his feet as he scrambled to keep up with her.

The girl wore a short black dress that cupped her ass, and she walked quickly, the thin fabric riding up until Paul could see the naked curve of skin. She glanced back at him, lifted her top lip to expose her teeth. A smile. Or what she thought a smile was supposed to look like.

Sweat beaded against him, clung to his pits and balls, and he could make out the smell of his own stink rising. Paul hoped the girl was far enough ahead of him that she wouldn't get a nose full. Once they got wherever they were going, he would find a bathroom, splash some water on himself. Fresh as a fucking daisy.

Ahead of them, the trees opened into a clearing, the moon suddenly much brighter without the cover of trees, and he squinted, his vision seeming to double.

The house in the center of the clearing had no door, no windows, but it had a roof and a brick front that someone had painted white but was now mottled with dark, bulbous stains that seemed to morph and change even as he watched. He thought again of the dark stain on the carpet back at his apartment; the stained flesh on the girl's face. He tried to follow the thread—to connect the dots—of each of those similar things back to some greater meaning, but as he watched the shadows lift and change, he lost himself completely.

Over and under they writhed, lifting and arching like bodies coming together, dipping in and out of each other. Fucking each other. That's what the stains were doing, and Paul giggled. Actually fucking *giggled* like some tiny-titted schoolgirl, and he clapped a hand over his mouth, but the girl didn't even toss a glance over her shoulder, and he dropped his hand.

If there was a way to actually get inside, he couldn't see it, but the girl kept walking toward the front, those stains rising and crashing, and he ground his fists against his eyes. Fucking Nathan, man. When he got back to the world, Paul planned on beating that piece of shit within an inch of his life and then finding another dealer. If he wanted his shit laced with the harder stuff, he fucking knew well how to find it.

Turning back to him, the girl reached out a hand and touched those squirming stains, and her other hand reached out to him, beckoned him forward. Again, those exposed teeth like a dog who knows it's about to be put down. A warning.

His stomach clenched, and he swallowed down the vomit forming at the back of his throat, forced himself to shuffle forward.

"Optical illusion," Paul said once he reached her.

The house wasn't a house at all, but a wall shaped like a house. Before it, a pit yawned wide and dark, jagged edges of earth crumbling away into candlelit emptiness that led down into something that never ended. There was no way that he could know that, but the thought came to him as he stared into it. This was a place in the earth that did not end, and now the girl stepped down into the pit, a series of stairs carved into hard dirt, and he hesitated at the top and called down to her. "Hey. Where does this thing go?"

The girl did not respond but kept on with her descent. Pausing, he placed his foot on the top stair then took it off again. His money. She had his money; he couldn't back out now. Not now that he had come all this way, and so he went down, the earth opening around him like a great mouth.

The air was cooler here, and he took in deep breaths of it. Drew it into his lungs until he coughed, the back of his throat gone raw and tasting of blood.

Candlelight flickered against black dirt, weak flame lit from somewhere deep within the bowels of the earth, and he watched the light trace ghost-like patterns across the packed soil. So much like the stains on the wall that pretended to be a house. He almost giggled again, but the girl's tight, bouncing ass kept the noise locked behind his teeth.

The stairs curved to the right, were cut deeper and narrower here, and Paul had to turn his body sideways, creeping along at

a snail's pace just so that he wouldn't bust his ass or break something on the way down to wherever the fuck they were actually
going.

Jesus Christ, he wished the girl would stop already, but she
just kept going, and he started to wonder if this was hell, and he
was going to spend eternity walking down a set of stairs that led
to fucking nowhere, but she stopped ahead of him and turned
left, disappearing around a bend.

"Follow me," she said again, and Paul stretched out his
hands to feel for the walls, stomped his feet against the dirt. Sure
enough, the stairs had stopped, and he followed the curving
path. Here the light grew brighter, and he hurried toward it,
catching a glimpse of the girl rounding yet another corner.

Dragging his fingers through the loose soil, he pushed his
frustration to the back of his mind. Surely this was part of the
buildup. Some kind of weird way of getting paying customers
all hot before unleashing an ungodly amount of pussy. A sales
tactic. Delaying the pay off. Oldest trick in the book. Same way
that dealers got people into harder shit. Sell the weak stuff first
and then tell them you have something that will blow them
away. The tease and the reveal. He was in the tease now. All he
had to do was wait for the reveal, and there had better be a
perfect pair of tits he could squeeze and then fuck at the end of
all of this.

The corner opened back up, a smooth tunnel of dirt
stretching on and on, but he didn't see the girl anywhere. Only
that dim light and the deep earth pressing in on him, and he
licked at his lips, which burned, and tasted of salt and beneath
that, something fetid.

"Hey," he called out, and his voice echoed back to him. He
waited for the girl to re-appear, that pale skin glowing, but she
did not.

Nothing to do but keep going. Nowhere to go but forward.

Even still, he felt stupid stumbling around in the dark like
some sightless mole pushing his way toward nothing. No, not

nothing. There would be a pay off at the end of this, and the thought made him hurry.

Around yet another turn, the path opened up into a series of vast rooms. Wide, arched openings stretched before him, and he moved past them, glancing inside as he went, but the rooms stood empty. No furniture. No beds. Nothing to indicate that anything had ever existed down here.

Who the fuck carved all of this shit out anyway? Someone had taken the time and the care to dig out some kind of massive, underground fortress, and it struck Paul that only an absolute nut job would do something so extensive for so little purpose.

Unless, whoever organized the Fleshtival had done it. Part of the appeal, but even still, it seemed like an awful lot of work for something that could have been done in somebody's basement or a rented house for just as much money. Hell, that was how porn worked, wasn't it?

His feet hurt. How long had he been walking? He pulled his cell phone from his pocket—no service, of course—but the digital clock told him that it was almost four in the morning. He and Jake had started driving at ten. He had lost at least five, maybe six hours.

"No fucking way," he said and checked his phone again. Half past five in the morning. He blinked at the screen.

Up ahead, someone laughed—a soft tittering—and he put his phone back in his pocket. The stupid thing was messed up. That was all. He'd get it sorted out when he got back home. Another voice joined the laughter, a husky whisper that made his cock twitch, and he smiled as he came around one last corner.

The corridor opened into what looked like an infinite cavern. Here and there, small niches had been carved into the dirt, and they stretched upward into a darkness that swallowed everything down.

Women lay inside of the hollowed out areas of earth, long

legs that draped over the sides, or arms that reached out to trace careful designs in the air, their mouths forming unspoken words behind bared teeth.

"Hello, Paul. We've been waiting. For such a long while." The girl who'd led him into the hole stood before him, and he licked at his mouth, shuddered as he felt his bottom lip split, blood spilling over his teeth.

"You left me," he said and hated the way that he sounded. Like a bleating, mewling schoolboy who'd shit his pants and needed his mommy to clean him up.

"No. We found you. Haven't you felt us? Like blood, like a stain, spreading over everything. We were there with you. Before you came to us," she said and drew him forward.

The women looked down from their holes at him, that same birthmark covering their cheeks or blotting out their eyes.

One of them leaned over and pulled her hair over her face so that he could not make out her features, and the thought flashed through his mind that perhaps there was no face behind that veil of dark hair, and he shuddered.

Above him, the darkness seemed to grow thicker. He could have sworn that he saw more of those little slots when he entered the cavern, but there seemed to be fewer now, and another woman—this one another blonde with mud streaked through the white strands—turned to him, her hands pulling her hair over her face as she did so.

One by one now, the woman tugged at their hair, covered their faces, and he whimpered, tried to drop the woman's hand, but she held on, her skin burning hot against his.

The room had certainly grown darker. Paul could only make out two, maybe three rows of those neat little holes.

"Listen, lady. I don't know what the fuck's going on here, but I left my buddy in the car. He's waiting for me, and if I don't come back, he's going to call the cops, and you better believe that they'll light this place up like the fourth of fucking July."

"No. He's gone now. He was gone the minute he came looking for us."

She turned to him them, those blonde curls hanging over her face.

He couldn't help it. He screamed.

When the darkness dropped over him, he tried not to listen to the sounds of skin scraping over dirt, the heavy breathing of those faceless women crawling. Tried not to feel their hair as it moved over his face, his chest; their fingers opening him up.

"We'll pluck out your bones and drain you dry," one of the women said, and the others sighed and moved over and inside of him, delicate hands and mouths creeping hot and sticky over his chest, his groin.

He drank of the darkness. The women fed him with their mouths, and he squirmed inside the dirt, everything melting away, and they wrapped him with gentle hands, guided him further into the ground, the soil soft and cool against muscle and bone.

"These are the ways you die. Learn them well. Take them into your mouth, your stomach. Let them swim in your blood. Some are punished. Some are not," one of the women said, and he opened his mouth to them, but they offered him nothing else.

For a long while, he cried. And then, he didn't.

The Beautiful Nature of Venom

When we met, you whispered in my ear, your breath hot, wet, and heavy with whiskey, that you wanted to know the feeling of my skin under your fingernails. There was lace around the collar of my dress, and I wanted you to take hold of it, rip it off of me, take my skin with it. Then you would see the spiders that live under my skin, the knife points of their legs splayed open like desperate women.

I turned away from you even though you couldn't see them. I wanted you to see them, wanted you to feel them slice through you from the inside out.

"What's your name?" I said.

"Doesn't matter," you said and laid a finger along my collarbone. Under my skin, the spiders traced the tips of your fingers.

"They're memorizing you," I said, but you didn't hear me.

"You want to get out of here?" you said, and I nodded. The spiders pushed against my skin, an obscene blooming in the darkness, and I brought my hand to my stomach, pushed their dancing legs flat.

"None of that prude bullshit for you," you said as we walked, and I let the clack, clack, clack of my heels answer you.

The spiders settled against my stomach, their legs fluttering like fans.

We walked slowly, and you wound your fingers in my hair. I like to think you felt them then because as they shifted under my scalp, you pulled backward, and I let a sigh escape.

"You like it rough, huh?" you said and looped my hair around your fist, pulled it towards you, exposing my neck.

"Back there," I said. Inside of my throat, the spiders threatened to split through my windpipe, but their sudden movement only jerked my head towards the empty alley just behind you.

You grinned, and your mouth was all wetness, your teeth covered by the slick velvet of your tongue. The spiders flooded my mouth now, clattered across my teeth.

I let you pull me into the alley, let you yank up my skirt. Your hands were rough, calloused, and they pulled at my skin. I could feel everything pulling away; skin from muscle, muscle from bone, and the spiders were singing, pushing against my broken flesh as you fumbled with your belt, your zipper.

Your fingernails pushed into my back, and I parted for you like the folds of tissue paper. If you held me up to the light, I would be translucent, a milky image of myself.

"Shit," you said and pushed deeper, and I stretched around you, my insides bulging as the spiders rushed towards you, their sighs whistling out from between their fangs. A sound so slight, so lovely, that I wanted to cry.

"Do you hear them?" I said, but your movements had become jerky, your breathing labored.

I wanted them to make you slow down, wanted them to let you hear them singing, but they could not. They were too busy. My skin swirled with the pinprick designs of their legs searching for an opening. I had become like a piece of lace, delicate and airy.

"I feel beautiful," I whispered to you as you finished, your fingers full of my skin.

"Fuck," you said and you leaned your head against mine.

Your sweat smelled sweet, and I brought my tongue to your cheek.

My own cheek burst open, and the spiders poured out, a beautiful glittering army in the night.

When you saw them, you smiled. For that, I think I loved you.

Like Feather, Like Bone

The little girl is under my porch eating a bird. Her hair is matted. She did not bother to push it back before she began, and blood has clotted against the white strands. I try to ignore her, but she is crunching its bones, and the sound is like the ground cracking open.

I creep under the porch, squat near her, but not too near. She still has her milk teeth, and they are sharp, a tiny row of pointed knives. Small feathers cling to her heart-shaped face.

"You shouldn't do that, sweetheart. It isn't good for you," I say.

"I want wings. Wings the color of the sky," she says and slurps at the bird's eyes.

"What's your name, darlin'?"

"Momma said I don't have one. But your name is Caitlin."

"How do you know my name?" I say, but the little girl shakes her head.

"It's a secret," she says and licks her hands, her small pink tongue darting in and out of the spaces between her fingers where the blood has dripped.

I feel I should take her inside; put her in a hot bath, wrap her in the thickest, fluffiest towel I can find, but it's her mouth that keeps me from taking her in my arms and carrying her into the house. She gobbles down a slimy string of meat, and I look away.

"Where's your Momma?"

"Under the water, under the water," she says, and her voice lilts up and down as if reciting a nursery rhyme. My skin blossoms into goose flesh despite the warmth of the late September afternoon.

"She went under the water. Like your Jacob. The sky doesn't go in the water. I want to be like the sky."

I haven't said his name in six months. Not since Colin left.

I pretended to listen as he spoke. "I'm sick of your fucking judgment, Caitlin. Like losing him didn't tear me open. Like you're the only one allowed to mourn. My boy. My baby boy in the goddamn ground, and I kept thinking that it wasn't right for him to be down there in the dark. He would be scared. Cold. It isn't right. I can't do it, Caitlin. I can't. " he had said. But I was happy when he left. He didn't know what it had been like to find Jacob, his eyes glassy, unfocused, his skin blue, his mouth filled with water.

"Jacob," I say and my mouth is full with the sound of his name. The little girl cocks her head, watches me, her eyes glinting in the shadows.

"Do you want wings, too?"

I think of the heaviness of Jacob's body when I pulled him from the water, my fingers scrabbling through his hair, dipping inside his mouth as if I could pull the water out of him.

I kneel beside the girl and watch her pluck the feathers from the bird. She gathers them in her hand one by one, and she laughs. It is like music, and I am so tired. I lie down in the dirt. It is cold and damp like the fistful of earth I placed on top of Jacob's small coffin.

The little girl hums, her voice high and quavering, and arranges the feathers around me. Her fingers are streaked with blood, but I do not care, and she places the feathers in my hair, tests their color against my eyes until she is satisfied. She pats my cheek, and her hands are sticky.

"There. Now you're like a bird, too," she says and resumes her song. Her voice is delicate, fragile, a thing I could take in my hands and crush. So much like Jacob's cold hands, tissue paper skin stretched across bone. So easily breakable.

Something flutters at my feet. A small sparrow hops toward us, its beak opening and closing.

"You're calling them," I say, and she snatches the bird, watches it wriggle against her grip before snapping its neck. The sound seems to echo against the slats of the porch, fills up the space. I think of screaming, but if I start I'll never stop.

She grins, her mouth all teeth and gore, and holds out her hand. The bird is still. I want to take it from her, breathe life back into it, but I remember Jacob, my mouth working to push air into his still lungs.

"Look," she says and turns, lifts her shirt to expose bare shoulders. "You see? It's working."

Dotted against smooth flesh are small bumps, dark specks against pale skin. Tiny feathers beginning to sprout.

Something sharp gnaws at my stomach. I am hungry. So, so hungry, and the girl turns back to me, places the sparrow near my mouth.

"Don't you want wings?" she says, and her voice is Jacob's voice. There is a roaring in my gut, an aching screaming to be filled, and I take the bird in my hand, bring it against my lips. It is so small. I do not think it will be enough.

"I can get more," she says. Behind her, small wings the color of the night sky unfold, flutter for just a moment before settling.

I bare my teeth, press them against warm flesh, tear at the soft feathers. It burns as I swallow. The little girl sits with me, sings her song into the growing night. Beneath my skin, my bones shift, and the dead make room for something new.

Worship Only What She Bleeds

The house bleeds at night. I know not because I have seen it but because I can *hear* it. The blood moving through the walls, a singular drumming heartbeat that presses against me, fills me up to the point where I think I might scream. But I don't. It wouldn't matter. The blood comes no matter what I do.

Momma tells me that there's no such thing as bleeding houses and that she ought to whip me for sneaking and watching *The Amityville Horror* even after she told me not to, but her ears are old, and she can't hear it. Not the way that I can. Every night the house pours itself back into the dirt. The blood finding its way home.

Even more than the sound there's the smell. A hot, metal smell. Like in the back of your throat in winter when you've been running and can feel all the raw parts of you exposed and open. It makes me sick. Plenty of mornings I wake up dizzy, my stomach heaving and rolling. Momma gets me on the bus anyway. Even the morning I threw up because the smell had found its way inside my throat. "Stop being so dramatic, Mary," she said, and tucked me into my green raincoat.

"A daddy would fix it. They fix things," I told her last night.

"You don't have a daddy anymore." She wouldn't look at me after that, picked at her bowl of lettuce and cucumber for an hour before tossing it in the garbage. Later, when I should have been asleep, I watched her pluck out her eyelashes one by one, transparent half-moons drifting toward the ground as she watched the mirror, her eyes unfocused, distracted. The blood roared through the house, and the stink rose, but she still didn't notice. I fell asleep watching her hands rise and fall against her face, the violence she committed there a small, quiet thing. In the morning, I don't ask her about it, and she doesn't mention that she found me out of bed, and we eat our toast in careful bites.

"I think," she begins but stops. She wipes at her lips with the back of her hand. A smear of red jam lingers in the corner, and she brings the same hand to my forehead, huffs as she sits back down, her swollen belly bumping the table. I think of the baby there, floating in the quiet dark. I wish I could trade places with him.

"You're warm," she says. She doesn't look at me, and her eyes are strange without their lashes, too big and wet, like massive pools of murky water threatening to spill over the shore line. A red scab has formed over her right eyebrow, and she scratches it, her fingers scrubbing against flaking skin.

"I don't feel warm," I say, but she shakes her head, her mouth turning down at the corners.

"You're sick. Very sick. A very sick little girl," she mumbles and scratches again at the scab. It looks bigger now, the size and color of a strawberry.

I reach across the table and pull her hand away. "You're sick, too. You could stay home, too. With me."

"It's just a rash. I'll put some ointment on it. I'll be fine." She pulls her lips back and grins. Teeth like an animal. Like Princess when we took her to the vet because she had to go to heaven. Like even though she was a dog, she knew something was wrong.

"Don't you want to stay home?" she says, and I nod my head. Outside, the morning light is covered in dark, and fog creeps against the windows like little fingers tapping. *Let me in, let me in.*

When she leaves, I hold my breath. Quiet. Quiet. Wait for the house to do something, for it to show that it knows that she is gone, that I am alone. But there is only the sound of my heart whooshing the blood to my head and a dull pain building in my lungs.

Maybe the house sleeps during the day. I try to sleep, too, but the fog rolls against the windows, and I can't settle down. It's too quiet and too loud at the same time. Instead, I turn on the television, but the fog has knocked out the antenna, and white and black ants crawl all over everything. I shut it off, and write my name in the dust covering the screen.

For a long time, I stand at the window and watch the fog. Wave after wave of white smoke crushing against the house. I press my face to the glass and cup my hands around my eyes to block out the light, but I can't see anything. It's like the house is floating away, the fog lifting and carrying us somewhere not solid.

"Where are we going?" I whisper, but there is nothing there to answer me. I want to go out into the fog, to float in it the same way that the house does. To be cocooned and protected inside of its breath. To sleep. Maybe I would forget the look on Momma's face when the police came to tell her about Daddy. Forget the worm crawling through the dirt I threw into the hole we put him in. Forget that he had been going to get ice cream for me. For my birthday. Forget that it was my fault.

Momma left the door unlocked when she left. I can't think of a time when she has done that before. She's always telling me stories about people who go around testing doors to see who's stupid enough to roll out the welcome mat for intruders.

"There's men out there just looking for juicy little girl bits like you, Mary. Looking for places to sneak in and find them and hurt them real bad," she would say but now the door is unlocked, and I want to float, so I open it and go out onto the porch. The fog licks against my feet, and I take off my shoes, curl my toes against the wooden slats.

Behind me, the door closes. It won't, I think, ever open again.

The smell lives in the fog now. Stronger than I ever, and I gasp against it, pull my shirt over my nose so that I won't retch. It worms against my skin, tries to open me up, little razors seeking something soft. It hurts, and I back against the house, try to get away. But the door is closed, and I can't go back.

The fog reaches grey fingers down my throat, twists inside of me until I gag, and I claw at the wood beneath my hands. *Let me in. Please let me in.*

The wood gives way, splinters into nothingness as I press harder, a hollow space yawning wide and warm. It's nothing at all to make it bigger, the wood breaks easily under my fists, and there is a hole large enough to crawl into, a place to hide from the sharp teeth of the fog. From somewhere deep in the house, the heartbeat starts up.

I creep into the space, careful not to catch myself on the jagged edges of the hole. The air here is softer, the smell not as strong, but dull, the reminder of a smell instead of the smell all by itself.

I should be afraid. Should leave here. Find a way to open the door. Go back to sleep and hope that I wake up when Momma gets back home, listen to the sharp sounds of her cutting vegetables, pulling meat from bone. But it's so nice here. So warm, and the heartbeat is like a lullaby.

Just like a little mouse, I think and giggle. Inside and outside at the same time. In the guts of the walls, under the floor. The hole tunnels forward, getting smaller as it goes on. I have to hunch my shoulders and duck my head, but the tunnel is just big enough for me to fit. I push myself forward.

My fingers brush against the edges of the tunnel, burrow

into piles of something soft. It feels like fur, like petting Princess, only it's longer and stringier. Like my hair when I haven't washed it in a few days and Momma practically pushes me into the shower.

It's wonderful to be inside the house, to squirm along just behind the walls, snug and safe where no one can see me. I have to hurry. Momma will be home, and she won't want me here. Will say it's strange to be inside the walls, and I don't want her to know that I found this place. She'll roll her eyes again; tell me that I'm imagining things. Like she did when I told her about the blood, about the smell. Like she always does.

She never *believes* me.

My hands are wet and sticky, but I don't know how they got that way, and when I push a clump of hair out of my eyes, something gets all gummed up in the strands. It's too dark to see what it is.

There's light coming from up ahead. Probably an opening into the house. Behind me, the tunnel is all closed up, and the fur stuff pulses and moves. I don't like it. I don't like that it's wet and looks like it's reaching out for me. I don't want it to touch me, to smear its damp fingers across my arms, my legs.

A round pinprick of light shines into the tunnel, and I stop my burrowing, stand before it, look out and out and out. I blink, shake the stars from my eyes, wet my lips with my tongue.

Momma's home. I can't see her from my spot inside the wall, but I can hear her humming. I don't know the song, and the notes don't sound right together. They're all jumbled up and screechy, and her voice slides over them like oil.

I'm inside the wall of her bedroom and can see her bed, the corners tucked tight and pillows propped just so. The dress she put on this morning is draped across the mattress, the shoulders placed across her pillow, as if she laid down and the bed swallowed her skin and bones and left the dress behind.

"Mary," I think I hear her say, but the words slip into something else, something that sounds like another language. The warm air in the tunnel has turned cold, and I shiver. The humming stops. Starts again. But it is different this time. Ghosts of words dance in the air, and I strain against the house to hear them. Underneath everything, the beating grows louder, and the fur stuff twitches.

When Momma steps into view, I scream. She is naked. Her legs bend impossibly, the joints crooking the opposite way, and she walks with slow, jerking steps. The scab on her forehead covers her face now. She's scratched at it, torn open the flesh, and blood drips across her neck and chest. Her mouth is open, a wide O, the tongue a fat, wet piece of meat, and her teeth are pointed and sharp.

She turns slowly, stares at the wall. Surely, she can see me hiding here, just behind the plaster. A small, quaking animal waiting to be gobbled up. She cocks her head and watches the wall, eyes flickering back and forth, nostrils flaring.

"Little pig," she says and grunts, reaches her hand toward my hiding place in the wall. I push away from the hole, but the tunnel has closed up even more, and the fur stuff snatches at me. Cold fear clenches my stomach, a grasping, hungry thing.

"Can you hear it, Mary? You were able to hear it before. Can you hear it now?" she says. From the other side of the wall comes the sound of her raking her fingernails across the plaster.

"The blood, Mary. I've always heard it. Come and see. Come and see," she says.

"Please, Momma. You're scaring me."

"Nothing's wrong, love. Come and see what I've brought you."

My face is wet when I press my eye to the hole again. Momma stands before me cradling a squirming bundle. She resumes her humming, and a tiny reddened hand reaches out, the fingers flexing.

"See what it's given back to me? To us? After all this time, Mary. A daddy. Just like you wanted. A daddy to fix things and to make everything better," she coos. A gurgling rises from the blankets she clutches to her chest. The sound of drowning. The sound of blood leaking from a cut throat.

"It's not a daddy. It's not. It's wrong," I say, and she bares her teeth.

"What do you know about it, girl? What do you know about the places daddies go? How they rut against you, their stinking meat between your legs? They all come in and go out the same way. Pushed out with the shit and the blood into the dirt, and they always *leave*. One way or the other. But not this time. It heard me. Heard *us*. Heard what we wanted, what we needed. And the blood gave back. Everything I've poured into this world, it finally gave back. Aren't you happy?"

The fur stuff has wrapped itself around my arms, my legs, and it pushes upward, envelopes me like a second skin. I don't mind any more. It's like velvet, soft and smooth, and I run my hand over the flesh sprouted new.

Inside the house, the new daddy cries, and Momma shushes him, brings him to her breast.

"Hush now. It'll all be all right. Everything will be all right," she says. I want to scream at her, to tell her to throw it away, to burn it, to cut it open and pour the blood back into the earth. But the house is in my throat now, the fur pushing further and further down, and I'm so tired.

Beneath me, the world opens its teeth, stretches its mouth wide as my body splits open, empties itself into the dirt.

The new daddy sings to me. His voice merging with the heartbeat of the house. The light fades. Blinks out. And I sleep.

The Tying of Tongues

When the hooded woman came to our village, her bloodied skirts trailing behind her, the old mothers whispered behind chapped hands, and the animals found their holes and hid.

"Shameful," my mother hissed and crooked her fingers against the woman's silent, creeping form.

"Witch," my mother called her and spat at the reddened twigs and grass she left behind. "Evil One. This is why she bleeds into the Earth. A curse for selling her soul, Anya."

I won't let Mother catch me watching. The woman's arms and neck are pale and smooth like the stripped flesh of trees. I want to take her fingers in my mouth like ice, like snow, let her skin melt against my tongue. But I cannot speak of this.

It is two days after she first appeared, and my brothers have taken me to the river. I tell Mother I am going to wash, but I love to watch my brothers fish, their fingers dipping in and out of the meat, their hands shimmering like starlight as they scratch away the scales.

We are alone this morning, and my brothers move about their nets carefully, their voices low. I watch the mist rise from the river and imagine stripping myself bare and walking into the water, the mist cupping my breasts, the waves lapping against my calves.

I drowse, lulled by the soft hum of dragonflies. My brothers notice her first; their stooping forms suddenly straightening, their murmurs falling into silence. They watch the woman in the same way that I do, try not to lick their lips when they see her figure moving through the trees. But they are caught up in their own visions and do not notice me.

"What would your wives say?" I say, teasing them. They smile without teeth, turn their eyes away but not their bodies. As she draws closer, our gazes land on her once more, all of us bewitched by the languid movements of her body. She moves like water, like wind.

I am not yet a wife, and my brothers see only what they want to see. I try not to smile as we follow the movement of her hips together.

"Where does she come from?" I ask, but they only shake their heads. Their wives have tied their tongues as Mother has my own.

"Perhaps if you looked like her, Anya—hair as black as the raven's feather, body like a ripe pear, you would not waste away in Father's house," Jacob the eldest chides me, and I try to blush, force the heat and color to my cheeks. It isn't so difficult with the woman standing near me, and heat crawls up my thighs, my neck.

My brothers laugh as I flush, assuming it is the fault of some toward village boy with wandering hands, but when they turn away, distracted by the possibility of biting fish, I glance again at the woman.

She is looking at me, her eyes so dark they almost blend against her pupils. Like looking into a night without stars. *Unnatural*, I think, but she appears amused, her lips lifting in the briefest of smiles before she turns her back and begins to move away.

I want to call after her, tell her not to go, but my blood has frozen, and I cannot.

But she is turning back, glancing at me once more, before moving into the trees, her skirts flashing crimson in the sunlight before vanishing.

My brothers have lost themselves again in the capture and kill, have turned their backs, and before they can notice, I slip away, the shadows swallowing me, sweet and cool.

She is waiting, and when I find her, she brings a finger to her lips and reaches her hand for mine. I hesitate. "Witch" my mother called her, but I want to know the feeling of her fingers in mine, so I wrap my hand around hers, and my mother's voice shimmers, falls away.

It is like touching glass. Like the sky has torn open above us, raining down fire and ice, and there is beauty laced with pain, and my skin stretches, full to the brim with her touch. I cannot bear it.

"I know you, Anya," she says and her voice is like birds singing into the gray morning, like wolves sending their midnight chorus toward the moon.

"Like honey. Like a flower. Something to be tasted. No doubt the men have come hunting for you, for that sweetness you carry between your legs?"

My head spins, the trees blur, become like some wide, yawning mouth. I fear I will tumble into them, be forever lost, but there is her hand pulling me back, holding me to this world.

"But I see your secret, Anya. It is written across your eyelids, it drips from your fingers, your lips. It takes no witch to see it," she pulls me close to her, her breath cold and wet. She smells of cloves and ocean water.

"Soon enough the men will begin to suspect. They will wonder why you turn them away, why they cannot lure you into their warm bed. And the town will whisper, will throw their barbed words against your back. You will bleed before it is done.

"I loved a woman once. But that was before the men came,

before they took us to the forest, filled us with sticks, rocks, their fingers. They pulled our insides into the night. So soft, so soft they said, and I held my love until she went still. Her mouth was full of leaves."

Her pupils dilate, all darkness and midnight. I think she will cry black, oily tears, but she does not. I weep for her instead, and she brings her tongue to my cheek. I wonder if I taste of salt or of something sweeter.

"They left us there. Food for worms. The vultures waiting to take the soft bits. But there were things moving in the spaces between the darkness and moonlight. Faces, hands reaching from under the trees, pale fingers full of death and magic. I let them take me, and they gave me back to the world. And it trembled beneath my feet like we had trembled beneath the muscled arms of those reeking men.

"They called me witch until I took their tongues, their children, pulled their bones from them one by one. Their blood rained over me, and I called it love."

I want her to press her mouth against mine, want to feel her moving against me as a husband moves against a wife, but she steps backward. The darkness seems to snake out from the hidden places in the earth. It swallows her, and I am alone.

I feel that I can taste her, the sharp tang of muscadine. I think of screaming into the sky or raking my hands across my belly, spilling my blood against the dirt. But it would not bring her back.

So I turn back to the river, to my brothers and their fish. As I walk, the birds drop out of the sky like stones and small woodland creatures lay down before me, their breath coming no more. I am not afraid.

MOTHER ASKS me to fetch water, so I return to the river. How the man follows me, I do not know, but he appears, his hand covering the place his wife should touch. I do not know him. He is not from our village.

He grins. His mouth is all wetness, and a deep fear flutters then settles in my stomach. I don't want him to touch me, but he is handsome, his shoulders broad, his eyes a clear blue, and I wonder if it will be easier since he is beautiful.

Because I understand what he has come for.

I could almost laugh at the absurdity of it all.

I try to run, but he is quick, his arms strong, and he captures me, presses me against the dirt. His smile is lovely, teeth like pearls glinting against the afternoon sunlight, and he brings them to my throat, traces his tongue against my collarbone, writes out his horrors against my skin.

I try to scream, but my mouth is full of leaves. I choke against them, and he laughs, smashes his fists against my teeth. My bones snap under his fingers, my blood caking under his clean, trimmed nails. He breaks me into pieces, uses the parts, the holes that he can.

He finishes, oh please let him be finished, and the sky is the color of blood. He kicks me twice, sharp blows against the ribs, before leaving, stumbling into the dusk.

Ravens and crows fling themselves toward the ground, and they fall around me, their feathers pointing toward the sky in rakish angles. Small creatures find their way to where I lie. They curl against my legs, my hands, sigh before they draw last breaths. I close my eyes.

I do not notice the hooded woman until she is above me. Her form blinks in and out, wavers between shadow and light. I think for a moment that I see dark wings behind her, the feathers deep and glossy against her bloodied skirts.

If she speaks, I do not hear, but the earth shudders under me, and she rips at what is left of my dress. Her mouth moves over me slowly, her tongue dipping in and out of the cuts he left. She moves down my abdomen, lingering in the hollows of my hip bones. Then she is breathing her secrets into me, filling my womb with words I do not understand. Curses or prayers to ancient gods swell under muscle, under bone. She speaks the language of trees, of wind, the humming truths of the river, and I am full, full of her.

"I'm dying," I whisper.

"Yes," she says simply. The growing dark morphs, disjointed forms taking shape. They creep across the ground, circle around us. Watching. Waiting.

"Can you love me?"

She touches her lips to my fingers, kisses them one by one.

"Yes," she says.

I close my eyes, wait for the shadows. We will wander the earth together, our blood seeping back into the ground, payment for what we have been given. And we will call it love.

The Marking

Violet woke up with the bruises. Outside, the sky had turned dark. A hushed grey filled with pinpricks of blue fire, and the world tipped forward, a great dome that would suffocate her if she breathed too deep. This was how it had always been.

Six this time. Six places where the blood pooled too close to the surface, the sick, purpled mottling blooming across pale flesh. She was hungry, but she would not eat. Beneath, her bones pushed against wasted meat. *It* didn't like when she went without food.

Her palm pressed tight against her chest, she traced her fingertips along her sternum, let them drift across the protruding rib bones. She counted them, wondered if with enough pressure, she could draw them out, release them from her thin cage of skin. If she did this, would it finally stop? Or would the marking linger on her decomposing body, a reminder even to the dirt that she was different, a thing separate?

Once, when she was a girl and the bruising had just begun, she'd found a slug and carried it home, her fingers aching from such a delicate touch. Later, she would eat it, taking small, neat bites. If she could fill her body with something else, something distinctly not Violet, perhaps the marking would pass over her, but the next morning the bruises had multiplied, and her mother smiled to see them.

How old had she been the first time? Five? Six? There were flashes of dark woods, the trees stretching jagged limbs against blackened sky, and the moon always absent. She could not remember it all. Hushed whispers, grunting. A great slab laid out before a hulking figure carved from stone. It would be years before she knew the correct word. *Altar.*

"Marked," her mother said each time, her fingers tracing the marred flesh. Over the years, Violet learned to hate her mother's touch, but she willed her body to hold still, to curl into itself, a small quiet thing in the face of her mother's fever bright eyes.

At first she had asked questions, but her mother would go silent, her eyes twitching away, searching for something beyond the physical space they occupied. But at night Violet listened. She tiptoed through shadow to her mother's room, pressed her ear against the door, and waited. If her mother ever dreamed of it, of the *thing*, its name never manifested. There was only silence in the great house, the rooms too large and menacing in their emptiness.

She would think of the woods then, those dark trees pressing down against her as she looked into the ancient stone face of something that had once worn the flesh of humans. But it had never been human. Even in her faded memory, Violet had the sense that it was much, much older than man. Older perhaps, than even her mother had ever imagined.

But she wasn't a girl any more. Had not been, in fact, for many years. She had moved out of her mother's house at seventeen, worked double shifts down at Fast Eddie's to cover rent on a shitty one-bedroom apartment that smelled of cooked cabbage and cigarettes. Somehow, fifteen years passed, but the marking never stopped. Starving herself seemed to keep it at bay, but the markings had begun coming closer together. What had once happened once or twice a year was now happening once a month. Fear curved like a hard stone in her belly.

Outside her bedroom window, the dark gathered, stars blinking out one by one, until there was only moonlight, and then that too was gone. In the corner, a darker mass formed, and then the sound of fingernails scuttling across hardwood floors.

"Violet." The voice filled the room, came from both beneath and above her. The shadow was on the ceiling now. Had it come from the window, or had it always been there, watching, waiting for her to finally notice its slow, calculated creeping?

"Hello, Mother," Violet said, and the voice chuckled, a deep, rasping wheeze.

"Never could fool you. Always watching me with those big eyes. Like you were drinking the whole world with them."

"I haven't eaten, Mother. For a long, long time." She offered up an emaciated arm.

"It doesn't matter anymore. Be a good girl and take off the blanket."

For a moment Violet considered not obeying, thought about running from the room to her car and driving until the tank ran empty or until her organs finally shut down. Flesh and bone mangled up with steel and rubber. But it didn't matter in the past. Certainly, it wouldn't matter now, and there was so little of her left. She had made sure.

She kicked at the quilt that covered her, pushed it down so that her naked form lay exposed. Warm, fetid air wormed over the soles of her feet, up and across her thighs, the concave bowl of her belly.

"Flesh of my own. Blood of my own," her mother said. The shadow was no more. Only her mother pressing against her, stretching her form to fit into Violet's. Her dark hair flowing across Violet's chest, spilling over her face. Their palms flat against one another, and then her mother's mouth forcing her lips apart. She smelled of earth, something that had come from beneath the ground.

"Feed me. This last time," she said.

⸺

THEY WERE IN THE FOREST. Breath coming in shallow bursts as they ran through the trees, branches tearing at their calves as they moved under a black expanse. Beneath them, stars burned, and Violet wondered if the world had come undone, if they had tumbled into the sky. Great white forms flitted in and out of the periphery, and the air lay heavy and damp in her mouth.

Her mother ran on all fours, her arms and legs impossibly long, the joints crooking upward. Violet wanted to scream, but she feared that if she did her mother would turn back, would look at her from a face that she didn't recognize. The thought terrified her. She kept moving. She knew the way.

The great stone loomed ahead of them, and her mother slowed. She turned away. She did not want to see its face.

"Look at Her, Violet."

Some animal cried out into the night, a long screaming that set her skin crawling.

"The Great Worm," her mother whispered and crept forward, curled herself against its feet, ran her fingers between her legs.

The statue leered down, the body and face of a woman, the mouth opening impossibly large, rows and rows of pointed teeth crammed into the space. A vortex of razor blades that went on and on. It was a mouth of violence. A mouth that hunted out soft flesh and attached itself there, suckled until it was satiated.

"From the beginning, She wanted you. Marked you as Her own, and She paid me for bringing you. She let me see things."

"Please. Don't," Violet said. She was so tired. She lay down, pressed her hands against the hard earth.

"There is a hole in the bottom of the world," her mother

panted, writhed under that gaping mouth.

"You know that moment right before you fall asleep? That moment where you can feel yourself falling? All that solid earth beneath you suddenly dropping away into nothingness? That's the hole opening. You're feeling Her move," she said.

The stars blazed, a piercing white light that bored into Violet's skull, burned ghostly images against her retinas. She clawed at her eyes, and her stomach heaved.

"And now, it's time." Her mother grasped at her, dirty fingernails pressing into pale flesh.

"Feed me, my love. My little daughter. Feed me now," her mother said, pressed her mouth to her abdomen. An unnatural heat that pulsated in time with her heart grew under her mother's tongue.

"It was you, wasn't it? It was always you. The marking," Violet said and wrapped her fingers in her mother's hair, tried to pull her away. Her arm was so heavy, and her mother was too strong. There was only the movement of her mother's mouth, the baring of teeth as she suckled, the burning as blood rose to the surface.

"She'll take me now. And the hole will open once more. Will open wide, and She'll take it all, everything tumbling into that great void until She's the only thing left. The way it once was. The way it should be. And I'll stand with Her as the world implodes."

Above them, the great stone eyes stared down, blank, unseeing orbs, and around them, all had fallen silent. Deep down, in the places where shadows slept, the world shifted, something great and powerful coming awake. Violet closed her eyes and let her hand fall from her mother's hair. Her mouth tasted of blood.

"These are the small ways we die, Violet. Every day, another part of us rotting. Bags of meat and bone. But you have fed me, have fed *Her*," her mother said, traced her tongue against Violet's skin.

The mouth opened then, the rows of teeth gleaming an unnatural white against the grey stone. The eyes looked down at them, examined the two women lying in the dirt. One crouched before the other, arms and legs tangled together.

When the entire world began to scream, Violet opened her mouth to add her own cry in the dark. Everything slipping away, land bleeding into sky, and something vast creeping toward the surface. She did not want to see, so she shut her eyes, closed them tight as she had when she was a child.

"It was always you. I didn't even know to hate you for it," Violet whispered.

Violet's heart fluttered against her ribs, a frenetic, broken pumping that hitched her breathing, left her gasping, her head a light, airy thing. For a moment, she floated, her body untethered from the earth, and she opened her eyes and *saw*.

Everything *she* had ever wanted. The large eyes of a small girl, her pale, fragile body stretched before Her, a vessel to fill. Rebirth. A doorway. And the dark haired woman so willing, so *eager*. She brought the girl, weakened her, marked her as Her own. And now, She would use the girl one last time.

"She never wanted you, Mother" she said and laughed. Whispered it again and again. *She never wanted you. She wanted me.*

"Of course She wanted you. From the very beginning," her mother said, but Violet shook her head, the effort knifing through her.

"No. It was only me. Only me. I can see now," she said. Above them, the blank orbs stared down, and the mouth opened impossibly wider.

"Too late. Too late," Violet said, and her heart shuddered, the speed too much to bear. Once. Twice. As the moment came, she smiled. There would not be enough left. Only a pile of skin and bone, a smeared reminder of what she had once been.

And then there was nothing remaining. Only a mother clutching her daughter to her chest as she screamed into a world fallen silent.

The Long Road

"It'll never leave you, Danny. Not now that you've heard them. Bet you can feel them itching down inside your guts. Bet you can hear them moving around out there at night. Sounds pretty, don't it? Bet it gets your pecker hard just thinking about it." Pop coughed, deep and wet in his chest, spit flecking gray stubble. He fumbled for the glass resting on the end table next to him, gulped at the brackish water he'd pulled from the marsh, smacked his lips and grunted.

"You thirsty, Danny?" he said, offering me the glass. I didn't want to answer him. Because I wanted that water, wanted to take it deep into myself, cool the burning working its way through my belly and down into my groin. But there were things moving in the dark liquid, things made up of shadow and night. Things that bite and tear and eat. I couldn't see them exactly. Could see only the outlines, the hint of fingers—or were they tentacles?—scrabbling, the slight high pitched hum of jagged teeth against glass, and I was afraid of those things burrowing inside of me, eating their way from the inside out. I shook my head.

"Suit yourself," he said.

In the night, I tried not to hear them. The beasts that moved. Long, slow undulations beneath the reeds that made me think of fish whipping their tails. Only there had never been any fish here. Pop dragged Ma here when she was fourteen, her brown skin stretched tight over the seed in her belly, and tied her to this place of rot. It took fifteen years for the beasts to come. They found us and spoke their words, their voices honeyed, and the world turned inside out like an animal peeled out of its skin.

Pop was the first to listen to them. *Walking the long road,* he called it. He took to the water like an alcoholic takes to whiskey, and before long his insides started seeping out of him, his blue eyes turning black and oily. Then Momma disappeared into the night, and the beasts ripped the sky open with their shrieking, and I knew the devil moved in that water. It didn't matter how much it burned, how pretty they sang, I wouldn't drink.

My tongue dried against the roof of my mouth, and Pop dragged his finger along the glass, suckled at the last few droplets. "You'll walk the road before too long, boy. And they'll be there waiting on you. Sure as shit they'll find you, crawl inside that pretty hide of yours, scratch that itch in your belly. Like the balm of fucking Gilead." And he laughed, his jaw working loose from the skin, the smell of his decay rising, hot and liquid.

And I was moving out the door, letting it bang behind me like the way Momma would have once hollered that I wasn't *raised in a fucking barn, Danny. We got some manners in this family.* Only there was no Momma any more, and I ran until my calves cramped, and I tumbled into the dirt.

Everywhere was the smell, the hushed whispers, and my skin blistering with the want, the need to drink of them. *This is my body. This is my blood.* The Holy Communion. The wafer and the wine. My body burning from the inside out, their voices scraping and sliding against my skin like claws and teeth hunting meat, but there was sweetness there, too, and the shame when I went hard, the shame when I pressed my body against the earth, spurting helplessly against the dust.

"Hard not to scratch that itch, ain't it, Danny boy," Pop said and moved beside me, knelt before the water, his hands twitching, dancing across the surface as the beasts unfurled, reached toward him. The fingers and hands of lovers.

He grinned. *Like the cat who ate the canary,* Momma would have called it. He had lost his molars, and he brought a finger against his right incisor, pushed and wiggled until the tooth fell into the dirt.

"Reckon I don't need them anymore, huh, Danny boy? The pipes are fucking calling, and shouldn't you be dead?" He paused, pushed against the left incisor until it too came loose then tossed it into the water.

"No, not you. But somebody you love. Somebody you love in the cold, cold ground, and you just keep on living, Danny boy. You'll push your lips against her grave and whisper to the worms, and that itch will just keep on gnawing at you." His eyes flickered, the darkness momentarily pulling away from something deeper.

Water leaked from my father's eyes, his mouth, dripped from what remained of his teeth. His lips coated with dark viscous dribbling, and his skin seemed to rattle, loose around his bones. His mouth opened, a great yawning chasm, and I could see the beasts reaching from his throat, groping at his tongue, as if the things inside were trying to find their way out.

"Come on and walk the long road, Danny," he said, and the things inside of him laughed, a deep gurgling that sounded like drowning.

And I ran.

§

I MET Sarah ten years later. While there were miles and years between, at night I'd dream of the long road, the beasts, and the water. Wake up screaming in the darkness, the mattress sweat soaked and cold.

I'd taken another girl to see Tom Waits. A girl like all of the other girls, the names vanishing as soon as they spoke them. She had spent the night applying and reapplying her too pink lipstick. Every now and again her hand would brush against my crotch. Pathetic attempt at seduction. Her brightly painted face like something you could look through and see the broken parts. Buried things she covered with the sharpness of her hipbones, with the emptiness of her sex.

I told her I needed a cigarette, left her sitting there, frowning at her own reflection mirrored in a lavender compact as she checked her lipstick once more. Vanity made flesh, and I moved away from her, through the sea of people into the spring night air that did not smell of salt but of pine.

Sarah was sitting on the curb, a dark sweater pulled tightly around her shoulders, the tip of her cigarette just barely illuminating the angles of her face. She looked frail, birdlike, as if I could gather her into my arms and grind her bones into dust. Her hair was cut short then, dark spikes tipped with crimson, the only color against her pale, clear face. She would tell me later that makeup made her feel like she was staring at the world from behind a mask, like what people saw was not really her but some approximation of her, a thing walking around in Sarah skin.

"So what are you running from?" Her voice startled me. I'd expected something light and airy, a voice to match the delicacy of her body, but the sound was deep and gruff. A voice steeped in long years of whiskey and cigarettes.

"I'm not running from anything."

She turned to face me. Dark eyes framed by tangled lashes. "That's bullshit, brother."

"Guess I could ask you the same question."

She inhaled sharply, laughed. "The same thing you are."

"I doubt that."

"See? So you do admit it," she said and stood. She was taller than I thought she would be, and she crossed her arms across her chest. It was a protective gesture, a closing in that prevented physical closeness. Much time would pass before she would unfold herself, and even then, her arms would be hard, her embraces too tight as if reminding herself that *yes, this is real, I have accepted this moment.*

We both went quiet then, smoked our cigarettes in the darkness.

"See you around," she said, flicked her cigarette into the bushes, and began a slow walk back to the building.

"What's your name?" I called after her.

"Sarah," she said and waved a hand in farewell, her slight form suddenly swallowed up. It took me two days to work up the courage to try to find her, try to figure out who she was, where she belonged.

She owned a florist's shop over on Midland Avenue, a small building of crumbling brick that I'd passed often enough to know the sign. I spent another three days driving past it, telling myself each time that I would stop, would go inside and talk with her, but I would speed by, afraid she would see me and think I was some creep.

Fucking do it, Danny. Just stop the goddamn car and walk inside. Tell her that you want to know her, tell her that you can't stop thinking about the things she said, tell her that you want to take her to dinner, to coffee, anything. Thoughts bumping against themselves, and my blood throbbing at my temples when I finally worked up the courage to go into the shop. Hoping she could be the thing to help me forget the house, the water, the beasts at the end of that long road.

"Looks like you aren't running away after all," she said, a small stone glinting in the curve of her nose. I hadn't noticed it before.

And I swallowed and told her the thing I'd been practicing for the past week. "Maybe it isn't running away. Maybe it's just taken me all this time to figure out what I was running to."

"You're fucking kidding me with that line, right?" she said and narrowed her eyes, but there was a smile curling at the edges of her lips, and I dipped my head, tried not to grin.

She taught me the names of flowers, my tongue tripping over the syllables, and at night when we lay in bed together I told her the stories locked in my head, the ones I knew by heart but was afraid to write down.

"You should do something with these, Danny," she said and pressed a hand against my chest.

"Maybe one day," I said, only I knew that I would never put them to paper. If I did, the world would come undone by its strings, and I'd be fifteen and on the long road again with Pop standing over me, his body dripping into the dirt.

"I'm serious. You're too talented to be stuck writing ad copy for some shitty, small time roofer."

"Maybe one day," I repeated, but then her mouth was on mine, and her lips tasted of honeysuckle and wine, and for a long while, I lost myself in the movements of her body.

When the nightmares took me, she didn't speak, didn't move until I came back to the world.

She only asked me about them once. "What are they? You talk about them in your sleep."

"It's nothing," I told her, and she pursed her lips, nodded. She had her secrets, too. A mother she never mentioned. An expired bottle of anti-hallucinogens tucked deep inside her bedside table drawer. A long vertical scar on her right wrist.

She filled my bedroom with flowers, and underneath the nightmare smells of salt and decay, the Carolina jasmine breathed its perfume into the night air, and slowly, slowly, the nightmares began to recede. The beasts becoming nothing more than shadowy figures, incorporeal wisps compared to Sarah's sleeping form, her breath warm against my chest. My childhood shrinking against what we called love.

Six months in, I wrapped a key to my place in an old watch box, lit some candles, opened a bottle of wine. She opened the box slowly, her fingers tracing the key's jagged outlines, her face expressionless.

"I'm sorry. It's too fast. Is it too fast? Just so you can get in if I'm not here, you know? You don't have to use it if you don't want to."

"Would you shut up for a second?" She lifted the key from the box, a momentary flashing of silver, and closed her hand around it.

"If you suddenly morph into some asshole, I'm cleaning this place out and selling all your shit on Ebay," she said, and I brought her hand to my mouth, pressed my lips to her fingers.

"Never."

She bought a delicate silver chain and wore the key around her neck; the metal nestled in the hollow of her throat.

"You shouldn't wear it there. Some weirdo could see it and follow you back here," I told her.

"You would protect me."

"Great. Have you seen me, Sarah? They'd probably rape me first."

"I like wearing it. The heaviness of it. It reminds me of you. Lets me know it's real."

It took another six months to save for a ring—a fleck of diamond in a thin gold band.

"It's a beautiful ring. She's a damn lucky gal," the saleswoman said and smiled, winking an eye smeared with one too many layers of kohl black eyeliner.

I told her we were going hiking. "Supposed to be the best weekend for fall color," I said against her protestations. There was a small mountain to climb, and when we crested the top, our breath coming quick and shallow, I gave her the ring.

"It doesn't fit," she said against her laughter.

"We can fix it," I said, and she pulled me deep into the forest, away from the trail. The smell of pine lingered in her hair for days afterward.

But then winter came and the nights grew long, cold, and she began to vanish inside of herself. It was like watching her disappear, like watching her become a ghost.

In January she stopped sleeping. She would lie in the dark with me, match her breathing to mine until I fell asleep. But when I would wake in the night, covered in the hard sweat of dreams, she would be gone, the place where her body should be cold.

I could hear her moving about on the roof above me, whispering to the stars, telling the faceless gods her secrets as she chain smoked, the cigarettes burning down to the tips of her fingers.

"It's nothing. I'll put some ointment on it," she said when I saw the burns. But each night she would leave me, find her way onto the roof, her voice floating down to me, words cut from nightmares.

"They found me once, when I was a girl," she told me one night in late January. There was snow, a light dusting of white over hard ground. "They came crawling out of the walls, made nests in my hair."

"What found you?"

"Can't you see them, Danny?" she asked, and her voice reminded me of Pop's, of the deep gurgling of the beasts, and I had the sudden desire to wrap my hands around her throat, to make her choke on the words she offered up like holy baubles.

"There's nothing there," I said, but she shook her head, turned from me, and moaned.

"They come out of the walls. Mother always said they come out of the walls. They want my skin, Danny. They want my skin."

I took her to the doctor, watched her as she took the pills he prescribed. But night after night, I could hear her moving above me.

"They won't leave," she whispered, and I held her tight, her bones like knives threatening to cut through her tissue paper skin.

When she split open the old scar, peeled back her flesh to let the things step inside of her, I found her too late, her blood blooming around her like the flowers she loved.

And I buried her, screamed what I had known was love against the frozen earth. *Old Danny Boy and his fucking pipes are calling.*

SARAH HAS BEEN dead for two weeks, and I am on the long road. It's certain what I will find waiting for me when I reach the end of it, and I listen for the beasts to begin their singing. Seems like I was always headed back here.

The old itch starts up in my belly, and from under the water, the beasts move, the smell of salt and decay thick in the air. I do not think of Sarah, only of the itch that needs scratching.

Pop is waiting for me in the house at the end of the long road. And when I get there, I'll take the glass of water he gives me. I have been walking for a long while, and I am so thirsty.

The Lightning Bird

Gable began turning into a bird at night two days after her mother died.

"Gable is a boy's name," one of the grandmothers said and turned her teacup in gnarled hands. A dark wart hung from her left eye, and Gable thought of snatching it between her fingers and dropping it into the tea that the group of old women, who had come to visit and help her mourn, requested that she make.

Gable had not wanted to make the tea, the itiye the old woman expected, and when she heard their slow footsteps on the front porch, she had thought of running, her legs tearing through the thick bamboo that grew up to the back door of the small bungalow she had shared with her mother for seventeen years. In the end, she had not and opened the door to their wrinkled faces that twisted into concern and sorrow when they saw her.

"Uma named me," Gable told them, and they clicked their tongues and shifted large bottoms against too small chairs.

It wasn't entirely true. Gable was her nickname. After her mother's favorite film star. Over and over they had watched the movie. Scarlett with her tiny waist and voluminous skirts, and

Rhett with a smile that Uma said the devil had sneaked inside of. A handsome smile. In this tiny Florida town far from their home of South Africa, it made Gable proud that she carried his name.

When she was born, Uma had gifted her a traditional Xhosa name. Lindelwa. The awaited. After the Inkaba, after the burning of the placenta and the umbilical cord, her mother had whispered her true name into the smoke, and had only called her Gable. She did not know how to be anyone else.

"It is a disgrace," another grandmother said.

"You're one to talk. Hair like a white woman," wart face said, and the other woman patted her platinum blonde hair that she had cropped short against her skull.

"I am an old woman. I can do as I please."

Gable turned from them and carried the pot back into the kitchen, but she could still hear their muffled voices worrying for her. Pitying her.

From the sitting room, a single word floated to her, and she brought a fist against her stomach thinking that it would keep her from unraveling.

"Amagqhira."

They would expect her to take her mother's place.

When the first dream had come to Gable, she was seven, and her mother held her tight when she awoke screaming into the dark. Uma did not scold Gable when she vomited over her mother's dress and the bed sheets, but smoothed her hands over Gable's face, and whispered to her. "It is like drinking the stars. Hard and sharp inside of your belly, and they burn and burn. You cannot keep them. The dreams. They must come out. No matter how good. No matter how bad."

No one had ever expected Gable to meet a man. No one would marry a girl so skinny that even the smallest dresses had to be taken in, and a face that was so dark, so plain. A face filled with darker eyes that seemed too large.

She would never be a mother.

"Your life will be the drums. The chanting and the music and the dreams. Bones in the dirt, and the people will come to you," her mother had told her that night, and Gable had swallowed the idea down, tucked it deep inside of herself like a beautiful jewel that only she and Uma had known about.

Now, standing inside of the tiny kitchen that Uma had kept scrubbed clean, Gable could not think of herself sleeping alone in this house. Day in and day out the people tramping dirt into the carpets and asking her for guidance from their ancestors over the stupidest of things.

Without Uma, the life that she had seen for herself since she was a girl rose up and choked her, dragged her down like a chain attached to her neck.

Setting the teapot on the burner, she waited for the water to heat. The grandmothers had not asked for more tea, but she needed to be away from them, away from their probing eyes and thinly disguised questions.

Again, their voices rose in the next room, and one of them laughed, a sly, high-pitched tittering that implied someone had told a dirty story. Probably about one of their husbands and how he couldn't get his pecker up.

Gable had heard variations of the same stories from the same group of women hundreds of times, and she had always been thankful that she would never be one of their kind. A used up woman with nothing better to talk about than her husband's shriveling penis.

The water boiled, and she dropped in the leaves and tried to ignore their snickering. She wished they would go away, leave her to the quiet of the house. She wanted nothing more than to sit in Uma's bedroom, lie down on her bed, the smell of smoke and incense thick in the room, and wait for the dreams that would surely come. The dreams Uma had promised her.

"Lindelwa? Our tea has grown cold."

Now that her mother was gone, she would never be Gable again. The grandmothers, the people of her little town would call her by her birth name, and eventually, they would call her something else.

Amagqhira. The healer. The diviner.

Gable went back to them and refreshed their tea. They sat with her until the first streaks of night slipped into the room, and then they each stood and patted her shoulders and cheeks as they made their way to the door.

"Goodnight, Umamkhulu," she said, and then she shut the door, listened as they shuffled away. She counted to two hundred, then five hundred to be certain that they had actually gone, that one of them had not decided to turn back, determined to stay with Gable through the night.

Had that happened, Gable would have run. Straight out the back door and into the dark stalks of bamboo that stretched green fingers into the night sky. Ran until the feathers began to sprout and her bones shifted to make room for something lighter.

Even now she did not know how much time she had left. Each night had been different. The first night she had woken halfway through the transformation and had been so frightened that she had hopped into the closet and stayed there until morning.

She had slept, remembered dozing off, but she had not dreamed, and in the morning, her legs were her own legs, and she had drank glass after glass of water, but she was still thirsty.

She'd spent the day wandering through the house, arranging and re-arranging the picture frames, the small wooden figurines of birds that her mother had loved so much, but her skin would not rest easy on her bones. For hours, she walked down the streets of the country she had come to know as her own. The country that her mother and so many of their people had adopted, but she could not settle into the cracks in the asphalt under her feet and came back to the house with its blue clapboard siding and white shutters and waited for night to fall.

Tonight, she threw open the back door and walked into the

bamboo. As she went, she unbuttoned the simple green shift she'd put on that morning, her shoes left beside the door, and walked into the darkness, traced her fingers over the dew that clung to her skin.

And she waited.

———

THE OLDER GIRL leaned over Gable, her eyes wide. "That isn't true. Uma told me," Gable said, and the girl threw her head back and laughed.

"Do you believe everything your Uma tells you, little girl?"

The older girl's name was Sisipho, but everyone called her Sisi. On nights when her mother went visiting, Sisi stayed with her. To make sure that Gable didn't get into any trouble, her mother said, but Gable never got into trouble, and she hated this girl who was only two years older than her fifteen years. Hated her for her soft hair and light amber eyes that crinkled in the corners when she smiled. Hated her for the way every boy, every man, would turn his eyes toward her swaying hips as she walked, her breasts straining against the thin dresses she wore.

"No, of course not. And I'm not a little girl," Gable told her, but of course she believed her mother. Uma knew things. Her dreams told her. The bones she threw told her. And Uma would not lie to her only daughter.

Uma had told her about the Lightning Bird, Impundulu, but it was not the fearsome creature that Sisi described. Her mother's eyes had gone soft and dreamy as she talked of a beautiful black and white bird that could be small enough to fit in the palm of your hand or big enough to fill the entire sky.

"Impundulu brings lightning. The rain. Gives us eyes in the night, lets us see the entire world opened up. A familiar. Impundulu has visited me, has served as my eyes. One day, it will visit you." her mother said and smiled a slow, heavy smile.

"Watch for him, Gable. You may wake to him in the night, a

beautiful man at the end of your bed, and he will take down the bed sheet, and lift up your dress." Sisi pinched at the tops of her thighs, and Gable slapped her hands away.

Gable left Sisi roaring in the kitchen and made her way outside. More and more frequently, her mother visited on the old grandmothers, held their hands and guided them from this world to the next. So many of them nearing the end of their time, and they called for Uma day in and day out, and Gable tidied the house while Sisi watched, made herself a meal that she did not eat, and then wandered through the bamboo until the moon rose.

Her mother had not talked about the black blood that Gable had found in the toilet. Uma had not had her monthly blood in a long while, and Gable was far from her own cycle. When she asked about it, her mother pressed her lips together and went back to her herbs.

"It's nothing, Gable," she said, and Gable had not asked again. She knew better than to press her mother to reveal something that she did not want to.

Gable had her own secrets. The darker visions that came to her, the ones that left her heaving with hot tears slipping into her mouth that she gobbled down. Fathers sweating and heaving over their daughters like beasts while mothers cowered in the next room, their hands clamped to their ears and a curse that would never come true on their lips. A son eating his meager breakfast and thinking of putting a pillow over the face of his mother, holding her there until her clawing hands fell slack, those terrible hands that would never rise to strike him again. She would not reveal them to Uma. Could not.

Uma's visions were of joyful things. Marriages. Births. Fortune. Her daughter's visions came with the darker tinge of nightmare, and when they came, Gable locked them inside and pretended that she had eaten something spoiled, that she needed to use the toilet. Nothing more.

"Some of us see the shadow world. Dream of terrible,

terrible things. But we are still the amigqhira. We do our jobs," her mother had told her once, standing in front of a large, boiling pot of soup, and Gable had cast her eyes downward even as her mother watched her carefully. If Uma knew, she never spoke of it to Gable.

Now, standing amid the bamboo, she closed her eyes, and thought of the drums, hard and heavy in her ears, her voice lifted to follow them, and her feet rose to match their rhythm. Her voice lifting into the old chants, the ones that would carry her spirit far from her body. The ones her mother had forbade her to use.

Out of the bamboo, above the house, she floated, followed the scent of her mother. Incense and oranges on her tongue as she followed her mother into a dark house, the sharp tang of citrus overtaken by the cloying smell of rotting flesh. Disease buried deep and working its way outward.

But it was not the older woman who smelled this way. Death had marked her. That was certain. Even Gable could see it from her place in the doorway, but the disease was in her brain, not in her body, and the decay that Gable smelled now came from her mother.

Uma turned and fixed her eyes on the spot that Gable occupied, and Gable fled the doorway, made her way back to her own body where she lay sweat slick under the green canopy waiting for Sisi to burst through the back door and tell her to come back inside.

When the girl finally did, Gable rose and made her way back to the house, gathering her dress against her as she went to ward off the chill settling deep into her flesh.

Her mother came in late. Gable heard her opening the door, taking off her shoes, before moving to the kitchen, and starting the burner for tea.

The door banged again as Sisi left, no doubt tucking the bills Uma paid her inside the small woven bag that she carried.

Gable pretended to sleep when Uma drifted past the door,

but her mother did not pause to look in at her as she had on so many other nights. Instead, she went on to her own bedroom and closed and locked the door behind her.

In the morning, they did not speak, and Gable sat at her mother's table and fought to keep from crying.

When her mother slipped a small black and white feather into the itiye she poured, Gable pretended not to notice and drank it down.

—————

IT WAS STUPID AND JUVENILE, and she should be ashamed, but she could not stop herself and flitted from house to house delivering her small gifts. These women with their barbed, gossiping tongues. They deserved something nasty.

The night air pulled at her, hard and insistent. The stillness in those enclosed houses and rooms stifled her, and she moved more and more quickly. If anyone were to wake, they would see only a bird, a blur of black and white feathers as it sought an exit, and then tumble back into dreams and forget.

Eventually, she found herself perched at the foot of a bed, staring down at the sleeping form of a young woman. Her belly swelled with child, and she twitched in her sleep, her hands pressed against the life that sparked there.

Gable did not remember flying here, to this house, and her mind searched back and back, but everything was dark.

Sisipho lay before her, and the girl reached out a hand to the opposite side of the bed. When she found it cold, found it empty, she withdrew her hand and frowned in her sleep.

Watching her, Gable felt no pity. Sisi had chosen poorly. A stupid, infatuated girl whose mother had to rush the marriage ceremony so that no one would see the slight bulge already appearing under her daughter's dress.

Gable crept closer and pressed her beak against the hot skin stretched tight. It would be nothing, nothing at all, for her to push against that membrane, let the blood rush into her mouth, hot and bitter, and drink until she was full.

"Impundulu," the voice said, and Gable looked up into Sisi's open eyes. Her face was wet.

"Please," Sisi said. "Take it out. Take it out of me."

Gable traced her beak down Sisi's abdomen, let it come to rest at the crest between her thighs, and breathed in. Salt and blood and sweat, and Gable was so thirsty. It would be so easy. So simple to take what she wanted.

From Sisi's inner thigh, Gable tore away a chunk of flesh and gobbled it down where it sank like a stone inside of her. She could not bring herself to take more, no matter how it eased the burning in her throat.

She left the girl she had once known lying beneath her and sobbing, her hands twisted around bedclothes gone dark with blood.

Until morning she flew without stopping and without awareness. There was still the taste of blood on her tongue like burning iron, and it was only when the sun finally rose that she slept and did not dream.

⸻

UNDER MOONLIGHT AND WEAK FLAME, Gable washed her mother's wasting body, gathered old blood in a wooden bucket and carried it into the bamboo, dumped it back into the earth. There kneeling under the sky, she would let herself drift into the darkness, her lips barely moving as she chanted, the tiny skull and vertebrae of a bird pressed into her right hand as she threw them into the dust.

"Save her," she whispered, but the ancestors did not hear, and every day her mother withered.

"I cannot do this," she said two nights before the last breath her mother drew. "Not without you." She could not tell her mother that she was frightened. Could not tell her of the nightmare she'd had the night before. Blood like a river flowing over their bodies. The both of them, submerged. Drowning. And the terrible bird, rising from the waters, its white feathers stained crimson.

Uma lifted her eyes, fever bright and rolling in their sockets. "Intombi. My little daughter. My little bird. Give me your hand."

Rising up onto her arms, her mother panted. "Not alone. Dream of me, intombi. Dream of me and bring me back," she said, and then her eyes fluttered backward, and she fell onto the pillow. She did not speak again, and in a day, her breathing slowed.

The old grandmothers found the two of them together, had to pull Gable away from the body, and still, she screamed and clung to the cold fingers.

"Leave us!" she told them, but they clucked their tongues and shushed her, smoothed her hair back as they whispered that it was better this way.

Gable let them bend and shape her body as they wished. Watched as their people streamed into Uma's home, watched them slit the throat of a goat that should have been oxen, and opened her mouth to receive the small portion of meat that was meant for her and her only.

The women had not left her alone that night, and she closed the door of her bedroom on their small sounds. Again and again Gable chanted, tried to catch at the sounds of drums, but sleep would not come, and her mother's body lay in the next room, a cold, rotted thing that would not rise again.

⸺

OUTSIDE, the sky turned black. Clouds piled one atop another, and she went to the kitchen and turned on the light. The faint yellow glow did little to chase away the gloom, so she turned to the window to watch the storm.

When the thunder began, her stomach clenched around the hollow Sisi had left, and she heaved. A thin line of drool fell from between her lips, and she sank to her knees, her fingers splayed before her, as the floor seemed to drop away and the back door blew open.

Again, her stomach contracted, and she gagged until a dark feather fell from her lips.

Taking it up, she smiled into the storm creeping into the kitchen. Lightning cracked in the distance, and the room flooded with ghostly light. The thunder drummed against the house, and she stood and gave herself over to the sound.

The heady scents of orange and incense flooded the small room, and she breathed them deep, took her mother's smell inside of herself and hid it away.

"Uma," she spoke into the lightning, and it was as if the lightning itself answered. The sound broke her wide open, and she sank to her knees under her dead mother's voice.

"Bring me back, Gable. Lindelwa. Little daughter with your dark dreams. Bring me back."

She thought the light would tear her apart, and she closed her eyes against it, but it still wormed along her skin, cutting against her with tiny, hot teeth, and she clawed at her dress, ripped at her hair. Everything burned and burned, but it was not beautiful in the way that she had always thought lightning to be.

Ugly and painful and ugly, and she could not escape, but there was her mother's voice, and she gave in to it. Sank into it like hot water, and her mother kissed her face and her hands, and Gable let her mother wipe the tears from her cheeks and the blood from her mouth, and there was no reason to fear.

Uma had died, had crossed into the place of ancestors, but she was here, with Gable, and it didn't matter how it had happened, didn't matter that it made no sense.

Cradled and safe, she followed her mother down into the dark, the places where Gable's dreams dwelled, and her mother fed Gable from her own mouth, and she ate hungrily. She drifted and dreamed, images of water and feathers and shadowed places opening their mouths, and the thunder coursed through her, the lightning burning inside of her veins, and she was again inside of the river of blood, but this time she did not drown.

"Bring me back, Gable," her mother said again, and the thunder stopped, and she lay on the kitchen floor, her dress torn to shreds, and her monthly blood between her legs.

Rising, she went to the sink, ran the water until it went hot, and then passed a rag beneath it. Carefully, she cleaned herself, and the water turned pink with her blood. When her skin was clean, she pulled her torn dress over her head and walked through the house naked. Here and there, she touched her fingers to a figurine, to a ceramic bowl, hard and smooth under her fingers, to the delicate lace embroidered along the bottom of the white curtains.

When she came to her mother's bedroom, she opened the door and moved to the old dresser, pulled a dress from the drawers, and tugged it over her head. It did not fit, but it did not matter.

With her mother's dress against her skin, she lay down on the bed, felt her blood come hot and thick between her thighs, and waited once more for nightfall.

⊏⊐

THE HOUSE WAS COLD, and the rooms smelled of stale air and the slight salty tang of unwashed bodies. Gable stretched her wings to their full length, allowed herself to fill the room. She did not have to hide, did not have to tuck herself away into small corners, a tiny, skittish thing that moved on the night wind.

The rooms were dark, and Gable made her way through the sitting area crowded with piles of clothes that stank and down the hallway where a lone door stood open. From inside came the small sounds of someone pretending to sleep.

Sisi sat up when Gable pushed herself through the door, the lower half of Sisi's face cloaked in shadow as if the dark was slowly gobbling her up. "Who do you work for, Impundulu?"

Gable did not need to answer her question. Uma's spirit burned through her like lightning, shook her heart like thunder. There had never been anyone else. Just the two of them moving through the shadow world, their dreams thick on their tongues, the hard angles of bones clutched against their palms, and the taste of incense lingering in their mouths. Mother and daughter together as one.

Gable went to the girl then, and Sisi lay back, went quiet while Gable, while the Lightning Bird, moved above her, the bloodied beak dipping in and out of that secret place that created life. A life that had not been wanted but now rushed inside of Gable like strong, clean water. The current of a river filling her up until she thought that she would stop breathing.

In the morning, Sisipho's husband would stumble home, his hands stinking of another woman's body, and all that he would find was the empty shell of the woman he'd been forced to marry.

The old women would gather and mourn Sisipho, mourn the loss of her child, and Gable herself would perform the umkhapho, blood running over her hands as she ensured the first step in Sisipho's descent into the world of ancestors.

Eventually, Sisi would appear before Gable in a dream, as the death ritual indicated, her teeth stained red, and Sisi would whisper that she was hungry. So hungry. And Gable would do what was expected of her—the amagqhira, the diviner, the healer—and guide her through.

ALONE IN HER mother's house, Gable waited. When the baby

kicked, she sang to it, all of the songs that Uma had taught her, and from deep inside, the child remembered who it had once been. Gable was sure of it.

When the time came, the contractions shuddering through her, she bit down on her screams and walked deep into the bamboo. Panting, she squatted over the earth and let the pain roll over her, lost herself inside of a darkness so deep that she wasn't sure she would ever break the surface, but then there was only a deep ache inside of her and the world filling up and everything stretching and tearing and there was only this moment, this bearing down, and the sky opening above her with brilliant light, and her blood rushing through her like thunder.

The girl child did not cry when her mother cradled her against her breast. Gable wiped the blood from the baby's face and brought her lips to the small, sweet forehead, breathed in the smell of citrus and beneath that, a smell of something much older.

Gable's daughter looked up with eyes the color of a deep river.

Eyes the color of dark feathers.

The Dream Eater

I don't remember anything before the field.

Momma tells me that I wasn't born here, that there was a time where I had seen something other than tall grass gone wild in the wind, but if that's true, I don't remember it. I can't even be sure that I want to.

"It was beautiful," she says and pulls a wet sheet from the basket at her feet, snaps it cleanly before hanging it on the line between us. I hand her another pin and don't say anything. It's better to lock everything up inside of me. Even if the words burn like acid deep in my stomach.

She hangs the laundry, and we don't talk about how the circle of red clay that surrounds our tiny cabin seems smaller, the long, green blades closer. We don't talk about the grass or the voices that come out of it in the night.

Instead, we finish the laundry, and I follow her inside where I pretend to swallow one of the meal replacement pills that are left in the white, government-issued bottles—Momma dry swallows hers—and we wait for the sun to set.

Momma sleeps, and I wait for the dreams.

I dream of the grass, verdant and cool on my tongue, as it

unfurls delicate tendrils down my throat. Dream of it taking root and spilling out from between my teeth and then covering the world. Everything bright and green.

I asked Momma once what she dreamed about, but she shook her head and pressed her lips together so that I could barely seem them.

I know what she dreams about though. The grass breathes her nightmares into the wind, and I catch at them and gobble them down until I'm so full I think that I'll burst.

The nightmares split open on my tongue. The forgotten taste of vanilla and burnt sugar. The smell of woodsmoke. Vermillion and gold and sapphire painting my insides. The colors of the old world. In my mother's dreams, there is no green.

I haven't taken one of the pills in three weeks. Momma needs them more than I do, and I haven't been hungry in so long. Not with the grass grown so high. Not with it creeping closer every night. For a long time, it stayed away from the house. For years and years we played keep away. When it started to move, Momma cried. There isn't anywhere else to go.

The next morning, I pull the old bucket off of the hook beside the back door and step outside. Fifteen steps should carry me to the well Momma's daddy dug on this land when she was a little girl, but there is the line of grass, and I'm still five steps shy of where I should be.

I leave the bucket and come back into the house. Momma stares out of the window, and I know what it is that she's seeing.

"Water's gone, ain't it?" she says.

"Yes," I say.

She turns to me, and the whites of her eyes are spidered with red. "We'll die without water."

I look down at the gaps between the floorboards.

"Take your pill," she says, and I palm it, put it back in the bottle when she ain't looking.

That night, Momma doesn't dream. There are things

moving in the grass, great beasts lifting terrible, beautiful voices in song, but they offer me nothing, and my stomachs shrinks into itself.

I fall asleep to the chorus of their voices, and in the morning my mother stands over my bed. More red lines thread through her eyes.

"Have you been out there?"

"No," I say.

She licks her lips and shifts from one foot to the other. A long time ago, a fox found its way to the cabin. Momma trapped it and kept it in a box with some holes punched through the top. Said that this was the last thing left. Other than us.

But there wasn't nothing to feed it other than the pills, and so it wasn't long before it died. She buried it, and I couldn't tell where the clay stopped and its fur started.

Momma looked like that fox now. Eyes rolling around and nostrils flared. Like I'd trapped her in a box with nothing to eat. She brings her face close to mine, and her breath is hot against my skin. It smells like old earth, and I try not to open my mouth to breathe it in. Momma wouldn't understand.

"They said it wouldn't come here. They said to take the pills and to wait. But it's out there. Isn't it? In the grass?"

I hold her hand while she cries. I can't cry for something I never saw, and all I can think about is the tinge of salt that will lay thick on my tongue when the grass brings me her dreams.

I don't get out of bed, and Momma stays with me, curls her body close to mine, a womb of bones. We drift in and out of sleep, and sometimes, she trails her fingers over my hair, and I wait. I listen.

We stay like this all day. Locked around each other until shadows appear in the corners of the room.

The sun has not fully set, and the grass is moving. It creeps on quiet feet, but I hold my breath, and I can hear it. I open my mouth.

Behind me, Momma sleeps, and she dreams, and I drink of

her. Those green whispers feed me until I can't take any more, and I gasp and heave, a thin line of spittle falling from my lips.

The voices never told me why they bring me the dreams, and after awhile, I stopped wondering because I crunch down on them, and they dissolve between my teeth, and they taste so *good*.

In the morning, Momma gets out of bed slowly. Her skin looks gray, and my stomach hurts with how full it is of her.

"It was so beautiful. When you were born. Before we came here," she says, and I can count her ribs through her shirt. "Be sure you take your pill."

"I've always been here," I whisper after her when she leaves. "Always."

I don't go out to see how the ring of red clay around the cabin has become so much smaller. Momma sits in the living room and watches that line of grass, but I don't join her. Instead, I trace the hunch of her shoulders with my outstretched finger and wonder what she'll taste like tonight. I hope that she'll taste of something green.

I want for her to sleep in my bed again, but that night, she closes the door to her bedroom and leaves me alone in the dark. I listen to her cry and wait for her to sleep.

She stays awake for a long time. I can hear her breath staining the air. Exhaling and inhaling, she doesn't sleep.

What lives in the grass screams. I do, too, but I don't think Momma hears me.

The next morning she doesn't get out of bed, and when I open her door, she doesn't move. Her breath hitches, slow and even, and I close the door.

My footsteps sound like nothing as I move through the cabin, out the door, and onto the porch. I stop dead in my tracks and look at the grass. Three steps off of the bottom stair, and I would stand in the middle of it. Stand where everything is thick and green and soft. I take my foot on and off the top stair and then look back to the closed door where Momma sleeps.

"Let her come, too," I whisper to the things inside of the grass, but it's daytime, and they don't answer.

All day long, Momma sleeps, and I starve. The grass can't bring me her dreams during the day. I watch her as the shadows steal into the cabin, and the sun turns the sky to fire.

The moment the last bit of light fades, her eyes snap open. "Did you take your pill?" she says. I nod, and she watches me with eyes that seem to understand my lie.

My tears taste like the memory of something burnt.

All night, she sits in the front room, and I grip the edges of my bed and dig my fingernails into the soft wood of the headboard. Anything to keep from bolting into the room and prying her lips apart. Anything to keep me from breathing in the honeyed remnants of her dreams and draining her until what's left is nothing more than a husk.

The things inside of the grass laugh and tap sharp fingers and teeth against the cabin. They are close enough to touch now. If I opened the door, would they come inside? Or would they wait out there in the shadow and the dark for me to place my foot back on that top stair?

I think they know what it is that Momma is doing. Sleeping when they sleep so that she can sit up and watch them move through the night.

Momma whispers, and I cannot hear what she says. The light coming through my window is green, and the color paints my arms and legs.

"Please," I say, but I'm not sure what I'm asking for.

"Come here, baby girl," Momma calls.

"I can't," I tell her, but she calls again and again, and my legs move on their own. I try to hold my breath so that I can't smell her, can't smell all of that green grass, but I have to breathe, and all of my air whooshes out of me. The smell of the dreams locked inside of her head makes me dizzy.

She stands when I come into the room. Her hands tremble, but she doesn't reach for me.

Outside, the grass steals up and over the porch. I can feel it just outside of the door, and my mouth waters.

"My daddy brought me here when I was a little girl. Said this was his sanctuary. That nothing bad ever happened here. He told me that whenever the world came crashing down around him, he knew that he could come here, and everything would be okay.

"I believed him. Even when everything died, and there was nothing left except for your tiny hand inside of mine, I believed him." She turns and looks out the window. "I was wrong."

Outside of the window, green shadows crawl all over. Momma picks up one of the pill bottles and opens it up. "These were supposed to save us." She puts the bottle to her lips and shakes it. Her throat clicks as she swallows until there is nothing left and then she throws the bottle against the wall. It clatters to the floor and the sound is so loud that I cover my ears.

"There hasn't been a time that we weren't dying slow. The world just learned how to make it happen faster. While we weren't looking," Momma says.

Something reaches out from inside the grass and touches the window. It looks like a hand, but at the same time, it doesn't.

My stomach clenches, and I bite down on my tongue hard enough to make it bleed. It's hot and tastes nothing like my mother's dreams, and I let it dribble out of my mouth and patter against the floor. A tendril of green reaches through the gaps between the floorboards, and pretty soon it's stained the color of my blood. The color of the old world. The color of my mother's nightmares.

"I'm afraid," Momma says when the window cracks all the way across. I thought it would be loud when the grass finally came into the house, but it isn't. It comes in soft and quiet, and still Momma turns to me, her eyes wet and her mouth stretched over her teeth. "I'm afraid."

I want to ask the things flickering through the grass to let Momma stay, but I am so hungry and their voices are lifting, offering me a taste of what I want. I think of Momma smiling, the morning sun streaming behind her and lighting up her hair so that it looks like she's made out of light. I think of her hands against mine the day that I cut my pinkie finger, the white bone gleaming underneath all of that darker meat, her voice calm and steady as she pulled a needle and thread through my skin. I think of the hitch in her voice when she pulls the covers tight against my chin and whispers that she loves me.

Momma takes me into her arms, and I can taste all of the things that I've never known on her skin: apples, and roses, and fresh bread. She cries and presses my body to her. "My baby. My girl. My little daughter," she says, and I look again into that green void.

It is only that. A void. And I am so hungry.

"Don't be afraid," I tell Momma, and I open my mouth.

Daughters of Hecate

Birdie kept a lone cigarette in her bedside table drawer for nights like this. Her hands shook as she lit it, and the slow blue pull of smoke through her lungs eased her shaking but not the fear coiled in her belly. In the glow, the streaks against her fingers appeared darker, as if the blood there had turned black, a clotted, poisonous leaking.

"What happened?" Dylan mumbled and shifted, the down comforter pulled tight around his chin.

"Nothing. Go back to sleep," she said and brought her tongue to her hand, traced it up and over her index finger and down into the soft flesh. There was none of the iron taste of blood but sweetness instead. Like an overripe date. Cloying and rotted.

Dylan rolled into her, his fingers grasping at her thighs, but she pushed him away. Within a minute, he was snoring again.

Three times now. She'd be dreaming of her mother's funeral, her legs frozen as she stood before the casket. Someone had covered her mother's face with a veil, all delicate bridal tulle and lace, and Birdie watched as the mouth opened, the red tongue darting forward and licking at the fabric. Searching.

Hungry. She'd wake with a scream dying in the back of her throat and blood on her fingers. Each time she hunted for a cut, a prick, anything that would explain the blood, but her skin was unmarked.

She believed in the power of threes. Her college roommate senior year, Livia, a girl who'd borrowed Birdie's toothbrush and taken large, groaning shits with the door blown open, had lent her a book titled *Daughters of Hecate: Reclaiming the Crone*. The book had gone on and on about the sacred nature of the female form and the power of the third embodiment of the goddess. How Hecate, the crone, personified the perfect feminine identity, how to tap into the power of threes through blood magick.

"There's so much more. Underneath our skin. Living and breathing and drinking in what it can. Waiting to be born. Waiting for us to gobble it up. There's power in that blood," Livia said one night after two bottles of Merlot. They'd turned out the lights, lit every candle they could find, even the plain white tapers that didn't smell like French vanilla or buttercream. Birdie had finished the book. Had wanted to talk about it, and this was how Livia insisted they do it.

"You've been going to that tarot reader again, haven't you?"

Livia shook her head. "You know, I can't wait to be pregnant. Get as fat as I want. I mean really fat. Big as a fucking house," she said, and Birdie laughed.

"You're so weird. You changed the subject," she said, and Livia grinned, her teeth stained crimson.

"You don't want kids?"

A deep hurt wrenched through her stomach, and she pushed a hand against her abdomen. Livia watched her, eyes rimmed in dark green eyeliner. In the muted light, her roommate looked dead.

"I did. When I was younger. But not anymore."

The truth burned inside of her like acid, but she tamped it down, ignored the sharp teeth of memory.

She wanted children. Wanted a little girl whose hair she

could braid in long plaits down her back. A little boy who would hug her too tightly, his love fierce and protective. But there was always the ghost of her mother, and the great fear that she would somehow fail those children. Leave them open and bleeding and raw and colossally fucked up. The way her mother had left her

"Did you see the pictures?" Livia said, and Birdie blinked, her wine soaked tongue moving slowly.

"What pictures?"

Livia was flipping through the book then, fingers moving impossibly fast until she stopped at a page Birdie was sure she hadn't seen. She'd read the book from cover to cover. It wasn't possible that she had missed a page, and yet, there it was.

In the back, in black ink, someone had scrawled out a series of drawings. A goat copulating with a bare-breasted woman, it's tongue extended like a proboscis and wrapped around her right nipple. A great worm devouring a blobbed, asexual form, its face upturned and smiling. The third image, however, had disturbed her. A nude, lank haired crone crouched on bare earth, the palm of her right hand pressed against the thatch of hair at her crotch. The other hand plunged up to the wrist into the rounded belly of another woman, her mouth open and screaming. Under the torn skin, an infant lay still.

"What the fuck, Livia?" Birdie said, and her roommate laughed, her head thrown back and throat exposed.

"I drew them. You don't like them?"

"No. That's some seriously messed up shit. Who draws shit like that?"

"Never mind," Livia said and tossed the book onto their faded orange coach. "Forget I showed it to you. It's really not a big deal. Just something I drew the last time I got high."

Even when Livia pulled her hair away from her neck, traced the curve of Birdie's shoulder blade with her lips, she could not forget the pictures. It was only when Livia pressed her fingers against the heat building between Birdie's legs that she lost herself and forgot.

The wine drew her under after they'd both come, sleep folding her into forgetfulness, and the next morning, the pictures were gone. When Birdie asked Livia about them, Livia looked confused. Told her that she didn't know what Birdie was talking about and could she please borrow that black dress for her date with Tonia tomorrow night?

But even now, when she closed her eyes at night, she saw the crone's eyes shining fever bright and the woman's mouth opening impossibly wide, the scream worming inside Birdie's skin.

She blew the smoke into the darkness of her bedroom, peered into it, looking for ghosts. If there was anything there, it didn't show itself.

§

"I've been having dreams about my mother. The same ones. Night after night," Birdie said. Dr. Nunnelly tucked an iron grey curl behind her ear and scratched something down on her notepad.

"Are they recurring? Different?"

"Kind of. It's hard to explain. It's like I know what's coming. I know that I'm going to see her, know that the veil is going to be there, but it's like I'm surprised every time, so it feels different. And I'm angry. Like really fucking pissed off that she's wearing a veil. But then I'm terrified. That's always the same." Birdie paused, fixed her eyes on the painting above Dr. Nunnelly's head. An older woman holding the hand of a younger woman. That's what Dr. Nunnelly was all about. Leaning on the support of other females. Letting your sisters guide you through life's thorny patches. All of that Sisterhood of Snatches Kumbaya bullshit. But her insurance paid, and after the fourth miscarriage, Dylan had thought it would be a good idea.

She'd found Dr. Nunnelly's website at three a.m. The dream had wakened her, the blood slick on her palms, and she'd cleaned herself up, gone to the kitchen and drank three glasses of water before opening her laptop and typing "miscarriage and hallucination" into her search engine.

Dr. Nunnelly's was not the first site listed but on the third page. She couldn't be sure why she bypassed the others, but the website name had caught her attention. *ThirdGoddess.net.* Something about Dr. Nunnelly's photo on the main page, her grey hair a mass of wild curls, her mouth set in a smile had felt comforting. Now, sitting in the office, her skin crawled, and she thought of running, but she stayed seated, picked at her cuticles instead.

"I hate that fucking painting," she said, pointing with her chin to the two women on the wall.

"The painting?" Dr. Nunnelly turned.

"Gives me the creeps."

"Tell me about that," Dr. Nunnelly said.

"I don't know. Just something about it feels off." Birdie knew that she was avoiding everything she had come here to discuss. She kept waiting for Dr. Nunelly to bring it up, to ask her the questions she expected. *How did you feel after the miscarriages? Were you sad? Angry? Did you ever think about hurting yourself? Someone else?* But Dr. Nunnelly let her continue to sit there and babble like an asshole.

"You mentioned your mother. Can you tell me more about her? Your relationship?" Dr. Nunnelly smiled, slow and encouraging. Birdie wondered if there was some special class where psychiatrists learned to smile like that. Soft lips, a brief flash of teeth.

Birdie barked out a laugh.

"I loved her. For a long time, I loved her. Because I didn't know any better. Because she didn't give me a choice." Her fingers twined through her hair, pulled the strands into small knots.

"But little girls grow up and realize that all of the things their mothers did as children, all of the things they thought were normal, were quiet forms of manipulation, of abuse. You see, doctor," Birdie leaned forward, placed her fingertips against the edge of the mahogany desk, "I've done all of this before. Talked to another doctor in another office. Learned all of the jargon that goes into classifying a narcissist. Gas-lighting. Triangulation. The Golden Child. The Scapegoat. Parentification and Infantil-isation. My mother was a self-absorbed, manipulative, bitch who denied everything she had ever done wrong, and I was glad when I put her in the dirt."

"Give me an example."

Squeezing her eyes shut, Birdie pushed her right temple. Behind bone, a migraine threatened to manifest, and she clenched her teeth.

"When I was seven, she told me she was divorcing my father. Told me that he was abusive, that he hit her. That she caught him one night in my bedroom trying to take off my panties. She cashed in the savings bonds my grandparents gave me when I was born. Five thousand dollars. Not much in the long run, but it was supposed to be mine. For college, they said. We moved away. Some shit hole that I never learned the address for. She went out a lot. We were alone. Me and my brother." Birdie paused. The re-telling of all of those old sins falling out of her like hard, wet stones.

"I found out later that it was my father who had left her. That she was fucking our pastor. One of the deacons. The youth minister. She ended up marrying the youth minister. Kevin. My stepdad. When I asked her about the affairs, she denied them." She wished she had another cigarette, but she had left her only pack in the car.

"She sent me to school without lunch. Figured I was smart enough to figure it out on my own. Wouldn't come to pick me up either. When I was a freshman in high school, I rode home with a senior boy who tried to get me to suck his dick. She told me it was because he liked me, and I should be flattered. My brother got the nice clothes. The attention. She went to his baseball games, his wrestling matches, his track meets. She missed my graduation. She made me feel guilty. Constantly reminded me how much she had sacrificed. Told me that I wouldn't survive on my own. She would do something and then deny doing it. She made me feel like I was crazy. Like I was seeing and hearing things that weren't there. Should I keep going or will that do it?"

Dr. Nunnelly pursed her lips, the pink edges of her lipstick crinkling, the line bleeding past her mouth. Whatever she was about to say, Birdie wished she wouldn't.

"I want to try something here, Birdie, if you're okay with it."

"Sure."

The older woman stood and moved out from behind her desk. Her legs slim and toned under a snug black skirt, an emerald green blouse artfully unbuttoned to reveal tasteful cleavage. The body of a twenty-five year old housing the mind of a fifty-five year old. Birdie wondered how much the good doctor had paid for her figure.

Folding herself into the opposite chair, Dr. Nunnelly extended her hands. "If you don't mind closing your eyes as well."

During the three years she had gone through therapy in her early twenties, her doctor had never touched her, had never come out from behind his desk. Hell, there were sessions where she wondered if he was even alive.

If Dr. Nunnelly wanted to hold hands, Birdie would give it a shot. She closed her eyes and reached out.

"Take a deep breath, Birdie. Focus on that breath. Notice the pattern of the air moving in and out of your body."

Hypnosis? Was she trying to hypnotize her? Nothing on the website had mentioned that Dr. Nunnelly specialized in hypnotism. But she settled herself, noticed the air moving in and out of her lungs, imagined it swelling her from the inside. A rounded place where a seed should grow but couldn't. She held onto that image, that empty place expanding with breath.

For long minutes, only the sound of her breathing filled the space, the pressure of skin on skin, the hands warming as they clasped together, and Birdie trying, as she had for the past year, to forget. To breathe.

"Birdie? Listen to my voice now. You said something earlier. Something I want you to think about now. That you felt that you heard and saw things that weren't there. Can you tell me about that now? About a moment where you saw or heard something that your mother said hadn't happened or didn't exist?"

Somewhere underneath the swollen silence in the room, underneath her breath leaking in and out, something long dormant broke loose.

"She always told me it was a dream. That I was just a little girl, and that I had dreamed it. But everything about it felt so real." Her breath came faster now.

"Vivid. I woke up one night, and something about the room just felt … wrong. And the smell. Like something dead but sweet at the same time. I sat up but didn't swing my legs over. Afraid of something reaching for me, pulling me under. My mother was in the corner, facing the wall. She was completely naked. When I asked her what she was doing, she turned around, and her eyes were gone. Not blacked out or rolled back in her head or anything. Just gone."

She didn't want to talk about this, but the words tumbled out of her.

"She was chewing something. Her mouth looked wet. I can't forget the sound. For years after, I would close my eyes and hear that sound of tongue on meat. It made me sick to my stomach, and if I puked, she came in and watched me clean it up, said that I was being ridiculous. She smiled, told me that I was dreaming, and to go back to sleep, and then walked out of the room. Only she went backwards, facing me the entire time. I was terrified she would come back. Stared at the ceiling all night listening for that sound, waiting for her to come. I had the thought that if she did, she would be on all fours. Crawling. Like an animal. The next morning she was completely normal. Didn't mention anything about what had happened, and when I told her, she laughed. Said I must have eaten something that gave me crazy dreams. It never happened again, and I stopped talking about it."

"But you remember it. You think about it. In small moments when everything is quiet. Maybe in those shadowed seconds between sleeping and waking. You remember. Don't you?" Dr. Nunnelly's fingers wrapped around her wrists, pressed against pulse points as if measuring her heartbeat. Taking note of the increased blood flow, the flush against the skin, the slight gasping as Birdie struggled to breathe.

"Yes."

"Dreams are funny things. You peel back the surface, every-thing external, and you peer down, and you truly *see*. The things that live in the dark. It can be so, so beautiful," Dr. Nunnelly's voice dipped low, a distended, bloated imitation of the voice Birdie had heard when she entered the office.

"I don't like this," Birdie said. Eyes snapping open, she pulled her wrists backward, but Dr. Nunnelly dug her fingernails into the flesh there and stared back at Birdie.

"We plant seeds. We feed ourselves on their withering. Your mother did it. And you've done it, too. It's just that some of us are hungrier than others. And you are so, so hungry. Aren't you?"

"Let me go," Birdie said and tried to tug at her arm, but all of her strength had leaked out of her like water. The room swam, Dr. Nunnelly's face doubling. One with that soft smile, the other with lips pulled back to expose jagged teeth. Birdie tried to stand, but her knees buckled, and she grasped at the edge of her chair, the fingernail on her pinkie splitting as she fell. Blood dripping against the white shag rug, spreading like some obscene blossom. Behind her, Dr. Nunnelly licked her lips.

That same, slow sound of suckling, of eating. She thought her head would collapse under the terrible pressure of that sound.

Again, her eyes fell on the picture, and the older woman's face suddenly changed. The face of the crone—the one in the hand drawn picture Livia had shown her long ago—leered out at her, her fingers wrapped in the younger woman's hair. Birdie would not look at the younger woman's face. She would not.

She feared that if she did, it would be her own face staring back, the mouth twisted into a scream.

"So much empty space. All of those places inside of us that we try and try to fill up, with men, with women, with children. Each of them sinking teeth into the softer parts, but they all tear away and leave the hole behind," Dr. Nunnelly brought a hand to the hollow in Birdie's stomach, the place that should be swollen with child.

Birdie drew ragged breaths, tried to swat away the doctor's hand. Everything inside of her burned, her blood, her lungs, her heart. All of the secret pieces of her laid bare.

"Stop."

"You bleed at night. Everything you've planted seeping out of you. Feeding you. Sustaining you," Dr. Nunnelly said.

Birdie bit down on the scream building in her throat and forced herself to her feet, veering for the door. *Run. Hide. Run. HIDE.* Find a hole in the earth and fill her nose, her mouth with cold, dank earth, and forget how to breathe. Cover her skin in mud and leaves until she vanished, became part of something older and darker than the warm blood beating inside of her.

Behind her, Dr. Nunelly laughed, and the door swung open into momentary darkness, and then the sun blazing hot and white, and Birdie couldn't see and stumbled forward onto the sidewalk. Before her vision faded came her mother's face hidden behind the veil, the red tongue pressed against the fabric.

§

DYLAN CAME to collect her from the hospital, spoke in low tones with nurses and doctors as they moved to discharge her. She'd hit her head on the curb they said, skinned her palms and legs on the way down. Thank goodness Dr. Nunelly had seen her fall and called for the ambulance. Several times, she'd opened her mouth to tell them. Tell them what? The minute the words formed on her tongue, she forgot them, her head left heavy and aching. They continued to bustle around her, removing small bits of gravel from her shins, wrapping her hands in gauze.

Finally, she and Dylan were alone in the car, the radio whispering the Ben Harper song she'd heard that day at the park, the week after the third time the doctor had told her that the tiny seed in her womb had winked out. It was the one that had left her sobbing, collapsed on the trail as a small crowd gathered around her, but the melody sounded disjointed, and she couldn't follow the words.

"Dr. Nunnelly," she began, but she didn't know what else to say. Her thoughts wisped away like shadows.

"I'm glad she was there. This could have been so much worse," Dylan said. He hadn't shaved that morning, and the dark hair on his chin only made his eyes look a deeper green. It had been the first thing she saw of him. Those green eyes looking back at her through the stacks at the Battle Hill University library. Three hours later, he told her that he already loved her, and she'd laughed at him. It took six months for her to realize she loved him, too. Livia had understood when Birdie told her about Dylan. They'd only fucked when they were drunk. It had never been anything serious, after all.

"I've been thinking. Let's take some time off. Go somewhere warm with sand and water. Drink tequila. Sleep in. Hit the reset button," he said, but his jaw was tight, the neck muscles corded and strained under pale skin.

It was like listening to him through glass. Or water. His voice stretching endlessly, the syllables bloating before coming to her as something alien.

She nodded, and he grasped her hand and squeezed.

"I'll wake you up every couple of hours tonight, okay? Doc said it was a mild concussion, but still. Better safe than sorry."

Her voice stayed locked in her throat, and Dylan drove on into the growing night, the dotted lines on the road seeming to vanish. Birdie wondered if the world had come untethered, if the gravity that held the two of them to this world had evaporated, and they had floated into nothingness.

He turned right onto Crescent, then left onto Grandin, and then he was helping her up the stairs, making her a sandwich that she tore into small pieces but did not eat. Time blinked in and out, the seconds a transparent thread that pulled at her heart, her tongue, until she felt flattened out, paper skin stretched over hollow bone.

Something she was supposed to remember. Something about Dr. Nunnelly. Something she had told her before she fell, but each time she caught at the edge of the memory it floated away, and she felt tired and told Dylan she wanted to go to bed.

Birdie watched the man she had known for eleven years flutter around her, pulling panties over inert legs, draping a worn Pixies t-shirt over her head and guiding her arms through. He did this silently, carefully. His fingers a series of light brush strokes against the numbness boiling under her skin.

He pulled the duvet over her, tucked it beneath her chin. A father putting his daughter to sleep. Tears pricked the corner of her eyes, and she blinked them away, settled into the quiet sneaking over her muscles. He didn't notice her silence. Turned out the light. Kissed her forehead.

She drew him to her then, her mouth seeking his. Her body suddenly consumed with some awakened, fiery need, and his fingers dug into the cleft between her legs, pushing her open as he fumbled with his zipper. He pressed his hardness into her, and it hurt and burned. His tongue languished in her mouth. A dead thing worth only its burial. And he pumped himself into her, everything she'd once hoped for spilled into something putrid and rotted.

"I'll wake you in a few hours," he said and kissed her forehead.

As he settled beside her, she waited for the dream. The afternoon disappeared behind a hazed film of memory, but the vision of her mother opened before her like a hungry mouth. Teeth snapping at meat. She closed her eyes and smiled. Her head weighted against the pillow, arms and legs leaden and immobile. Somewhere in the dark, a tongue extended, a slow suckling that she remembered from the dark of her childhood.

Her stomach heaved, and she took the shadows of the room into her, breathed deeply until there was nothing left. Her mother would be here soon. The veil would drop, and her mother would rise, her arms strong and fluid, and gather her daughter to her bosom. Flesh begetting flesh.

"We all plant seeds." Her mother's voice, rising from the dark.

"You took everything I had. Everything. Give me this one thing, Mother. Please."

"I always knew you were hungry. My girl. My little daughter. You eat them up. Pull their blood into you until there's nothing left. Our children."

"Stop," Birdie said, but her mother's voice floated to her, strong and clear.

"We've always watched you. Knew that as you fed yourself, you would feed us. Make us whole. Make us strong. We have waited for you. All three of us. For so long."

The sound of nails against wood as Birdie looked up, watched as her mother crawled on all fours across the ceiling, her mouth drawn into a smile, her eyes missing. Then her mother's face morphing into Livia's. Then, Dr. Nunnelly descending, drawing her teeth along Birdie's throat, her belly. Planting her seed. All the same. One body. One thought. The blood between her fingers. So sweet. So clean.

Birdie brought her palm to her abdomen, pressed against the small, squirming thing pushing outward. She drank her tears down and whispered her lie into the dark.

"Shhh," she told her unborn daughter. "It's alright. It will be alright."

Birthright

My sister was the second. I was the first, but I never told Mina that. She would have been angry even though she didn't understand.

"A woman. Skin the color of the night. Her eyes and lips cut out of stars. You saw her, too, yeah?" she said, and I sighed and rolled onto my side, the pale yellow comforter tucked under my chin.

"You think you're a poet or some shit?"

"No. I just saw her. That's all."

Mina was two years younger than I was but already looked older. Breasts swelled under the T-shirts she wore and her eyes were a pair of dark irises without spark set inside a darker face. I'm not sure when it happened. When her face became like a dead thing made animate so similar to my own.

"Didn't you see her, too?" she said, and I didn't want to tell her yes; didn't want to tell her how Momma had come to me more times than I could count, dead lips pressed to my ear, feather light, as she whispered the secrets she'd gathered like flowers from the place beyond.

"Go to sleep," I said, and I listened as she rustled under her sheets and sighed. If Momma wanted me to tell her, she would have said something.

"Can you sing? For just a little bit?" she said, and because I was tired and because I knew she wouldn't let me sleep if I didn't, I sang into the darkness, the notes melding into damp, summer air. When Mina began to snore, I dropped off.

"Momma," I said even though Mina called her the Dark Lady, but Mina was so little when Momma died, and she didn't recognize her when she came. Even if Mina remembered her face, she wouldn't have known her. That terrible thing that had come to nest in her lungs had metastasized, had eaten her up from the inside out, and then her skin couldn't hold all of the rot in anymore, and she died.

I should have known better than to call for Momma. She never came when I wanted her, so I leaned back into my pillows and thought about how I could get Shane Connelly to notice me during second period and how to get Mina to think that it was an angel come to watch over us and not the thing I thought it was.

I watched the ceiling, dark shadows elongated and bloated into strange shapes, and listened to my sister shift and moan underneath the weight of the nightmare, and I could taste the edges of it. The dark stains that seeped into waking. The ones I recognized from the patterns traced on my closed eyes. For the hundredth time, I considered that it wasn't Momma who came to us, her tongue tied up by silence, but some darker thing that found a hole and crept through.

I slept. My dreams unfolded like petals, delicate and pink, and Momma came to me and touched my face and hands, and her touch was soft as moss, but her eyes were bloodied and her skin had gone slack and pulled away from bone. A body long hidden under earth. I wanted to shrink from her, wanted to moan and curl away from the cup of her touch, but she was my mother, and her hands on me were gentle, and I could feel my sister sleeping in the bed next to mine.

In the morning, there were dark circles under Mina's eyes, and she didn't look at me as we dressed for school, and we ate our bowls of cereal in silence. Dad was already gone, rising in the dark to dress. Some mornings he'd come in and stand beside our beds, his feet shuffling so he wouldn't wake us. I'd pretend to be asleep. Sometimes, I could hear him crying.

Mina pushed her cereal to the edges of the bowl and drew her spoon through the pale milk. "I heard you last night. Moving around in my dream. Like a click-clack, click-clack. And the Dark Lady ran away when she heard it," she said.

"It was just a dream. We're going to be late. Finish your cereal," I said, and she looked up at me, and something moved behind her eyes. A shadow or a dark unfurled wing or antennae. An insect like crawling that skittered across the surface and then vanished.

"Little pieces. She took little pieces. Gobbled them up and swallowed me down," Mina whispered, but I pushed her words away, and ignored the aching in my lungs and belly. Fear come to nest inside all of those soft organs and meat.

"Hurry up," I said and placed my own bowl in the sink and headed outside. By the time the bus finally pulled to the curb, my shirt clung to my back, and my hair had begun to frizz. I slicked it to my scalp, but it didn't help. Mina didn't sit with me like she normally did but moved to the last seat in the back of the bus and leaned against the window.

I took our normal seat and kept my palms pressed against the foul smelling, brown leather, my teeth clamped against my tongue, as I thought of my sister's words. The dream had changed. The nightmare had taken a new shape, and I didn't recognize it, and there was a burning inside of me because it had changed for Mina but not for me. I imagined the feel of Momma's mouth against my skin, how it would feel to have her tear away at this useless skin. To grow into something else.

"It isn't fair. I was the first," I said, but the sound of shouted voices drowned me out, so instead I bit my thumbnail and forced myself to not turn around to look for Mina. No one sat with me, and so I spent a few minutes pulling at the bits of skin around my thumb until the skin went raw and bloodied, and I stuck my finger into my mouth and sucked.

I couldn't help it. I turned around. Mina sat with her face pressed to the window, and again I thought I saw something reach out from her hair. A proboscis extended and hunting for soft flesh, but the sun flashed through the glass, and I winced and then there was only Mina, her hair pulled back from her face as she stared out the window at the early September Georgia bleeding past. A riotous death rattle with teeth choked in green and on the precipice of rot.

Mina didn't look at me when the bus pulled up to school but rushed past, her head tucked down, and I waited for everyone else to leave before I stood up. The driver watched me in the rearview mirror, his face weary. Like he just wanted me to get off the bus so he could have some quiet.

"I forgot something," I called and hurried back to my sister's seat. I dropped down so the driver couldn't see me and traced my fingers over the worn material, but I didn't know what it was I was looking for, and the seat was slick under my hands, so I rose and stumbled past the driver, my face in flames when he saw my empty hands.

First period was boring. An hour of listening to Ms. Adams drown on and on about the Russian Revolution, and I kept picking at my thumb, squeezed it and watched as the blood beaded against the desk. Five, then six drops, and I smeared my fingers through it, drew a heart in the stain and then scribbled it out. Shane Connelly watched me, but I couldn't stop myself. His face was calm. Smooth. I burned under all of that indifference, but my hands swooped up and down and my blood smeared over the desk, and the air was thick with the hot smell of iron.

At lunch, I looked for Mina, but she wasn't in our usual seats by the window, so I sat alone and picked apart the chicken fingers the school system called healthy. I had my head down when someone sat next to me, and the air filled with the smell of sweat.

"Why were you doing that?" Shane's voice is low, a whisper scraping past his lips, and I froze.

"Doing what?" I said even though I knew what he meant. I wanted to hear him say it.

"With your thumb."

"I don't know. Bored, I guess."

He paused and glanced down at his hands. There was dirt under his nails and ground into his cuticles. "Yeah. Gross though," he said, but his face was still, and I didn't think I believed him.

"Yeah. Sorry."

"It's okay."

My mouth was open before I could think. Words poured out of me like water, and I tried to press my hand to my mouth to keep them back, but it didn't work. "I have this dream. About my mother. She died when I was five and my sister was three. Car accident. Ever since then, my sister and I have had the same dream. Every night."

"You miss her?"

I shrugged. "Probably. I think I do. It was such a long time ago," I told him, but the lie tangled in the back of my throat, and I coughed into my hand.

He took my hand between his, turned it so that my thumb pressed flat against his palm, and my breath hitched. His hands were rough, calloused, and his skin caught at mine, and I wanted his flesh to hook against me so that we were part of the same beating heart.

"She won't ever let you go. You'll drown inside of her. She'll split you open and plant herself inside of you, and your heart will tear in two, and she'll eat those parts that are best." He dropped my hand and stood. I was left clutching my hand to my chest over the place where I thought my heart should be, blinking at the hundreds of dark legs creeping over Shane's neck. I didn't call him back.

The rest of the day blurred together, and I waited for Mina outside the bus, but she never showed up, and I rode home alone. She'd done that before. Stayed after school for tutoring or to make up a test or quiz and then caught a ride from a friend, but her absence stung in a way it hadn't before, and I folded my arms over my stomach and pressed down so that the emptiness there wouldn't hurt as much. It didn't help.

The house was quiet as I let myself in. The clock in the kitchen ticked out the seconds like a long thread, and I stood there and watched the second hand crawl over the numbers and wondered if Momma had ever done the same. Stood under the watchful eyes of that clock and questioned how it was she'd come here and what slow end would belong to her when life came winding down, a burial shroud borne in its hands.

Room to room, I wandered, my feet leaving a track through the dust, and I looked for Momma. Looked for the Dark Lady, but I could not find her. Not in the waking world.

Our bedroom was too warm, and I turned on the ceiling fan, so that the air moved sluggishly through the space. I went to Mina's bed instead of mine, her laced, pink quilt crumpled at the foot, and I slipped beneath it, pulled it over my shoulders and closed my eyes. If Momma came, imagined that the daughter she found in the bed was Mina instead of her eldest, perhaps I could steal away the dream that had belonged to Mina. A birthright returned.

Sleep did not come. I turned my face into Mina's pillow and breathed in her scent, and bared my teeth against the fabric and screamed until my throat ached. "Where did you go," I said, but Momma wasn't there, and the house stayed silent.

When the front door opened, I pulled the covers over my head and waited for Mina to come into the room. "What are you doing?" she asked.

"You don't deserve it. I was the first."

Mina didn't respond but sank onto the mattress next to me and twisted her hands against the cover. "Was there ever a time you wished she wouldn't come?"

"No."

"I did. Would hold my eyes open until they burned, but she'd come anyway. Every night, her mouth open wide. Hungry. But she never did anything but press damp fingers to my skin and moan. There were never any teeth to the things she brought."

"But now ..." I said, and Mina brought her fingers to the comforter, a ghost touch over my mouth, my eyes.

"I don't know," she said and lifted the comforter, pushed her body into mine. "Stay here. Until she comes," she said.

"Okay," I said and together we waited for sleep to descend.

When the dream took hold, I could feel Mina against me. The hard weight of her body a tangible thing that tied me to the Earth, but there was another part tugging me upward and away, and I followed it.

When I woke up, I tried to remember the dream, fought to hold the wisps of it in my hands, but it bled away, and I knew that Momma hadn't chosen me. Behind me, Mina slept on, and I left her there and crept out of the room. Dad must have come home and went to sleep because his door was shut as I passed it, and I paused, pressed my hand to the doorknob, and turned. Locked. I pressed my lips to the door. "Are you afraid of us?" I whispered.

Perhaps the Dark Lady came to him, too. She'd be with him now, ingesting pieces of him so that he could never leave her, and I wanted to kick in the door, to scream and scream until the dream broke and then take all of the things she'd gifted him. Even though I loved him. They weren't for him. They weren't.

"Take me, too. Please," I said and thought of Mina's face. So much like my own. So much like Momma's.

"She heard you again. Ran away," Mina said and I turned. She crawled on all fours, her hair pulled over her face so that I couldn't see her eyes, and her fingers dug into the carpet. She'd taken off her shirt, and there was blood on her arms and chest, and she lifted a hand and traced a heart in the spatter. Her muscles flexed and shifted, and she opened her mouth, and there were the undulations of dark legs. An insect caught in her teeth.

"She didn't," I said, and I thought of my own blood spread over the desk. How it must have turned black by now if Ms. Bregeth hadn't cleaned it. Wondered if Momma bent to taste it, if it would be the same as Mina's. Skin begot of skin and blood begot of blood. If she would recognize it as her own.

"Yes," Mina said and pressed herself into the floor, the blood smearing against the carpet. In it, I thought I saw something move, and my stomach turned over. "I'm tired. She won't let me sleep."

I stepped over her, left her lying on the floor, and went back to our bedroom. Her voice an undercurrent to the night sounds of the house, and I clamped my hands over my ears. "Fuck you," I said, and Mina's laugh was filled with the sound of underground things that crept on many legs.

In the morning, Mina was gone, the indentation her body left gone cold, and Dad's bedroom door was open, the bed made and his pajamas mounded on the floor. I poured a bowl of cereal but didn't eat it and then dumped it in the garbage. If Mina came home, I wouldn't let her inside. I was the one who carried the key. If Mina wasn't there, Momma would have to come to me.

When the bus pulled to the curb, it gave two quick honks, and I hid behind the curtain, watched as the driver peered at the house, and then drove away in a cloud of black smoke. I thought about trying to go back to sleep, but I wasn't tired. There were pills that Dad had taken after Momma died, but I didn't think she would come to me if I took one. Or if she did, she would be all messed up, and I still wouldn't have what I wanted.

I turned on the television. The woman on the screen looked too much like Momma, her teeth exposed, so I turned it off again. Something flickered across the screen, and I stood and pushed my fingers through the dust, but there was nothing there. No paper wing or jointed mandible waiting to snap at my fingers. I wiped my palms against my jeans.

I drifted in and out of the rooms, took inventory of all of the things that were supposed to make up our lives. All of the things Momma left behind when the earth swallowed her and how we'd tried to glue them back together.

I left the door open when I went outside, the cool shadows of the house spilling over the back porch, and wandered the fence line, my fingers tripping over the split wood so that it splintered, caught against my fingertips. I didn't bleed. I wish I had.

Mina was crouched in the corner, her hands plunged wrist deep in dark earth. "Help me," she said, and I didn't think as I bent to help her claw open the earth. Her breath leaked out of her like something sugared. Syrup or some other cloying thing.

Our hands turned over bits of rock, worms squirming under our fingers, and our breath came fast, the rise and fall of our chests a singular movement. A small hole opened beneath us, and we cupped our hands full of warm earth and drew it out into the sunlight, but it didn't mean anything, and I was so tired.

"She's here," Mina said.

"No. She isn't anywhere. She's fucking dead, Mina. Momma's dead, and there's nothing that's going to change it. Nothing. She's dead." My voice was a scream lifted into the afternoon sunlight. The birds kept right on singing, and Mina stared back at me. It was like looking into a mirror. I raised my hand and brought it shuddering down against her face.

The sound was enough to make me wince. The sick slap of bare flesh against bare flesh, and Mina didn't pull away or put her hand against her cheek. She didn't even make a noise.

Mina smeared her hand over her mouth so that the dirt clung to her skin, and she reached over to me and did the same.

"She's here," she said again, and something pressed outward from under her skin, reached out to me, but I kept myself still. If I touched her, I would kill her. My hands that had memorized her body because it was my body, would know the thin places to rip and tear, and I would have opened her up and fed her blood to the worms at our feet.

"Stop sneaking into my dreams. She doesn't like it," Mina said and rose, turned her back to me, and walked back into the house.

I spent the rest of the afternoon taking the worms between my fingers and crushing them, their multiple hearts bursting over my hands. I licked at the smears they left on my skin, my tongue tracing up and over the bare flesh. They tasted of nothing. I wondered if that's what I tasted of, too. Wondered if that was why Momma hadn't changed the dream yet.

When Dad's car pulled up into the driveway, I was still in the backyard. His door opened and shut, and I heard him come into the house, heard him call for me. For Mina. When he came through the back door, I didn't sit up.

"Where's Mina?"

"I don't know," I said, and he sighed. Like I'm always supposed to fucking know where she is. Like it's my responsibility.

"I got a call from the school," he said, and I rolled onto my side and waited for him to stop talking. I heard him shift, take his hands out of his pockets and rub them together. "If you're sick, you have to tell me, okay? You can stay home, but I need to know. In case you need me to stay home with you or to go to the doctor or something."

Fuck off, I mouthed.

"Listen. I'm trying, Hayley. I really am. But you have to give me a shot," he said, and I wanted to tell him I was sorry, but I didn't. The door clicked shut, and I lay under the sky until it went dark and then got up and went into the house.

"There's dinner if you want it. You just have to heat it up."

Dad sat at the kitchen table, his own food untouched, and his fork laid across the plate.

"I'm not hungry," I said and left him sitting there. Once, we'd had family dinners. The memory was hazy, but I could see Momma in her place, her face frozen in a smile, her lips stretched back and back and back, and Dad beside her, his eyes cast down.

Mina was in our bedroom. She'd stripped the blankets off of our beds and mounded them in the center of the floor space, and she curled inside of it, her eyes locked on something I couldn't see.

"Look," she said and lifted her shirt. Her skin was drawn tight over her ribs, and something squirmed underneath. "She's coming through."

"Stop it," I said, and she scratched at herself, her fingers digging until she began to bleed. I should have stopped her, should have taken her hands into mine and forced her to be still, but I couldn't move, and Dad came into the room and started shouting, his hands fluttering over Mina's body as he tried to push the blood back inside of her, and I sat down on the carpet and watched as he wrapped her in a blanket and carried her out.

Dad drove us to the hospital without talking. Mina gibbered in the passenger seat, her tongue lolling and her teeth clacking, and I picked at the frayed edges of my shorts and pressed my knees against the back of her seat. Normally, Mina would have turned around and hit me, told me to knock it off, but she faced forward, those strange syllables leaking out of her, so I stopped and drew my legs up into my chest.

The waiting room smelled of mold and antiseptic. Dad had gone back with Mina and told me to stay put, left his wallet in case I wanted something from the vending machine. A television blared in the corner. Some show where people stuffed their fat, little sausage bodies into spandex and ran through an obstacle course. Their grunts echoed through the empty waiting room, and I stood and turned off the television. No one came out to tell me I couldn't or to turn it back on, so I picked up a magazine and sat back down.

Someone up front laughed, and the sound of low voices carried through the empty space. I pulled two of the chairs together—the cracked vinyl scratching my face and hands—and laid down. Again low voices floated from the front of the waiting room, the murmurs like soft tongues singing, and I closed my eyes, and then I was in the dream.

Momma stood behind me, her hands braided through my hair, but I couldn't see her, couldn't turn my head, and she hummed, something high and lilting, and I leaned into her.

I waited for the dream to change. For the dream to be Mina's dream, but Momma hummed, and everything was the same, and I couldn't move. My lips formed around all of the words I wanted to speak, but there was no air inside my lungs. Parts of me cut out like a paper doll. She hummed and drew her fingers through my hair, but she didn't scrape her teeth over my skin.

When I woke up, my hands were wet, and I wiped them against my shorts and sat up. The room was silent. The women at the front still sat, their shadows playing out across the floor, but their murmurs were gone. I scrubbed at my face, touched my hair, but my mother's fingers remained a part of the dream.

I looked again at the shadows that resembled the women, and I couldn't remember if I'd seen the shapes before, if they'd stretched over the floor like that, their necks and heads deformed. They didn't move, didn't twitch or seem to breathe, and I forced myself to stand. The floor felt spongy beneath my feet, as if it would drop away if I didn't move carefully, and I went to the entrance and paused. The shadows still sat there, and I counted to ten. My heart ached from beating, but I counted again to ten, and then stuck my head around the corner.

There was nothing there. No women fallen asleep with their

heads and arms gone slack or still as stones as they stared at their computers. Their chairs were empty, and the computers cast a dull glow. I ducked back into the waiting room. The shadows stayed where they were.

I turned the television back on. Better to hear annoying chatter than silence, and I settled into my chair. I waited.

Three hours later, Dad still hadn't come out, and no one else had come in. I didn't want to look at those shadows, to see if they were still there, still unmoving, and so instead I watched the television.

When the woman who looked like Momma came on the screen—her face covered with a dark veil—I rose and went to stand in front of the television.

Behind her veil, she grinned, and her teeth were broken and stained, and they gnashed against the fabric, her hands pressed flat against the dress she wore. She wasn't my mother. This woman with her wide mouth. She wasn't my mother.

Click-clack. Click-Clack. The noise came from behind me, but I watched her, and the noise grew louder.

"Come out," I told her, but she shook her head.

"It's mine. The dream. Why won't you bring it to me? It's supposed to be mine," she said, and her eyes rolled in their sockets so only the whites showed, and I pressed my face close to hers, breathed in the dust and waited.

When the doors opened, I shrieked.

"Let's go, Hayley," my father said. His right arm was wrapped around Mina, and she leaned against him, her eyes heavy and half-closed.

"Have a good night," the receptionist said as we passed the front desk. She did not cast a shadow.

Dad buckled Mina in, his hands careful and slow, and then he pressed his lips to her forehead, and my heart surged. "I'm sorry," I said, but I didn't say it loud enough for him to hear me. Maybe it was better that way.

"They did a CAT scan. Of her brain. Doctor said he

couldn't see anything odd. Nothing out of place. Said maybe she was overtired or looking for attention." Mina sat next to him and didn't move, didn't respond. Still as a doll, and Dad reached over and patted her arm. "Said to let her get some rest. They gave her a pill and said it wouldn't take long. You'll probably have to help me carry her inside."

I should have told him not to let her go to sleep. I should have told him lots of things, but I sat there in the backseat and let him drive us back into something we couldn't have understood.

When we pulled up to the house, Mina was asleep, and together, we carried her inside, and laid her on the bare mattress. Dad found a clean sheet and draped it over her.

"You okay?" he asked, and I nodded.

"Yeah. Just tired."

"You get some rest, too. You both need it," he said, and I thought he would pull me to him, thought he would kiss me on the forehead the way he used to when I was a little girl and Momma was still here, but he smiled and then left.

I stood over Mina, watched her chest rise and fall, and cupped my hand over her mouth. Her breath streamed over my palm. Easy and soft.

"Are you dreaming? Is she there yet? With you?" I said.

Mina's eyes were the color of rainwater when she opened them. Unblinking as she stared past me at some fixed point I couldn't see.

"She wears the crown. They pried her apart with their hands, burned the pieces, the shards of bone, but she's still there. Momma saw her. At the very end. And then the light went out." She reached for me, and I bent, let her put her arms around me, and she shook. We sat locked together that way, two sisters clutching at something that our mother had seen and tried to lay at our feet. But she hadn't understood what it meant when the Dark Lady came to her and spoke those promises in her ear. She saw only the clear faces of her daughters, and she'd opened her mouth and said yes.

"What do we do?" Mina said.

"I don't know. She won't come to me. Won't let me see her."

"Don't let me go to sleep," she said, and I hugged her to me, felt the quiet beating of her heart against mine.

"I won't," I said. Because Mina wasn't the first. It wasn't hers to take.

When the sun streaked across the ceiling, Dad knocked on the door and opened it. "Mina, honey? I made a doctor's appointment for you. Just to make sure you're completely okay."

Mina brought her lips to my ear. "Don't fall asleep," she said and stood. She was still in the clothes she wore yesterday. Dad placed a hand on her shoulder as she walked past, and then he looked at me.

"Can I stay here?" I asked, and he nodded.

"Get some rest. There's bread for toast if you get hungry." He paused, lifted a hand, and then put it back on the doorknob. "I love you," he said and closed the door behind him.

I listened for the sound of the car starting and then went to the window, pressed my face against the blinds and lifted the edge of a blade so I could watch as Dad backed the car down the driveway.

"I love you, too," I said and their faces disappeared, blurred impressions of eyes and mouth, and then I turned back to Mina's bed and lay down. "Momma," I said even though I knew it wouldn't be her when the dream took hold.

For a long time, sleep wouldn't come. The morning was bright against my eyelids, and I pulled the blanket over my face, but it was too hot, and so I pushed it off and stared at the ceiling. The plaster circled outward in never ending rings, and I followed them, tried to find the place they ended, but my head started to hurt. I closed my eyes again and counted my breaths, tried to find the moment where my lungs emptied out, tried to feel what it was like to be hollow, and then I was in the dream.

The deep acrid smell of something burnt filled me up, threatened to split me open, and I coughed. A hand twisted against my back, and the smell grew stronger.

"You were the first," the voice said, and I knew that it was her. The Dark Lady.

"Yes."

"Your sister. She was the one to find me. Your face in miniature. Your mother's face. That dark root inside each of you like it was inside your Momma. Already twisted in your blood. You've felt it already, haven't you?"

"Take it out. Please."

"Can't," she said, and her hands were black and red, and her tears fell into the dirt and sizzled. "So many things I've taken out of the women who came to me. So many wriggling creatures drowned or pulled squalling into the air. Cut them out so their husbands and fathers wouldn't break them open, their blood vermillion and burgundy on those pale hands. So many things I gifted them. Taught them how to keep their babies inside of them, how to bind up their wombs so they could hold onto the things they wanted so desperately but would pour out of them over and over. And they came and they thanked me. By the time your mother saw me, it was too late. What was inside of her was too deep to rip out. What she had to offer was so small."

She licked her lips, and the skin blistered and cracked. "Three women. All bound up in diseased blood and bone." Her hands threaded in my hair, and I leaned into her the same way I leaned into Momma. "I had a little girl, too. They took her and filled her mouth with earth. I could still hear her cry at night, and I'd wake up with my arms empty, and I wanted nothing more than to cut my own heart out, but there was nothing sharp in the place where they put me."

Her fingers burned against my skin, but I didn't pull away, didn't run. "Please," I said, and she sighed, her breath like the wind or cold water moving quick, and she tugged at my hair. I winced, but I stayed still.

"Your mother said the same. Your sister, too. So many with that word pasted on their lips as they lifted their hands and asked for things they didn't understand, and then I did what they asked, and they clawed against me, begged me to take it all back. But when something's asked for, there's no changing it. Do you think that your mother knew what she asked for? Do you?"

I looked down at my hands. I wanted to say yes, wanted to tell her I understood, but my skin prickled, and I thought of Mina, her whisper still heavy in my ear as she told me not to go to sleep.

"You don't," she said and her words died in the air, and I was alone.

I opened my eyes. Deep inside my chest, something twisted, and I could feel it moving through my blood. Spider like. Fanged. Delicate legs fluttering and then growing stiff as they solidified. I pressed against my breastbone. "How long have you been there?" I said, but I already knew that it had always been there, just like it had always been in Momma.

I threw the blanket off and stood. Dad wasn't back yet and so I went into the kitchen and made some toast. I took two bites and it sat in my stomach like cardboard, so I threw the rest away, turned on the kitchen tap, and pressed my mouth to the stream of water and drank until I gasped and pulled away.

I went outside, knelt beside the hole Mina and I had created, and dipped my fingers into the dirt. The thing inside of me reached out, too. A paper chrysalis unfolding to reveal the tender meat beneath. I used my fingernail to scratch numbers into the earth. Ten. Twenty-seven. Thirty-five. Counted out the possibilities of how many years would pass before that chrysalis turned dark and then unfolded sharp wings.

"What did you ask for, Mina?" I said, and the sun beat against my back, sweat working its way between my breasts, and the grass seemed to shimmer and drop away, the heat inside my bones, and I breathed in, exhaled, and the grass withered beneath me. Full summer dropping into decay, and I felt the moon beneath the world, the full weight of her and how the sun pressed down and down, and how she burned with her own quiet heat, and I understood.

I didn't need to ask. I knew what it was Mina asked for; knew the price of what such a thing cost, and the dormant, hungry blackness inside of me reached out to its like as it curled inside of my sister. From deep beneath the hole we put her in, Momma reached up, too.

When I heard the car pull up, the sun was already sinking, and I stood and went back into the house. Dad helped Mina up the stairs, and she looked up at me. I nodded, and she pushed her hand against her mouth—a brief flash of teeth—and then her eyes focused on the stairs in front of her.

Dad helped Mina to the couch, and she tucked her knees to her chin. She looked so small. He turned on the television and handed Mina the remote. "I'm going to go get you some water so you can take your pill. Just rest," he said and left us alone.

"It'll get dark again. Won't it? We'll spend the rest of our lives waiting for the sun to set," she said, and she lifted her shirt to show me the mark spreading like a bruise across her chest.

"Waiting to sleep. Waiting to wake up."

"Look," Mina said and pointed to the television. "You see her?"

A reporter faced the camera, her face serious as she held a microphone. Behind her, a small crowd of people milled together, their heads leaning as they spoke to each other. Only one faced away from the camera, her back hunched, and her hair long and tangled with leaves. We knew her—my sister and I —and Mina reached for the remote and turned it off.

"What did she tell you," I said, but my sister turned away, her dark hair streaming behind her, and Dad came back into the room.

"Here. Take this. It'll help you sleep," he said.

"Don't," I said, but Mina had already tipped her head back, the glass in her hand as she drank in long, messy gulps, the water spilling over her chin as she watched me.

"Good girl," Dad said as she handed him the glass and sank back into the couch. Behind me, the television turned back on, but the remote was on the floor where Mina had put it. Dad didn't notice, but turned and headed back to the kitchen. "Try to get some rest. The pill should help," he said, and Mina watched the television. I didn't turn around.

"She said she could smell it inside of me. The same smell that Momma had. Festering and ripe. Said she knew how to cut it out."

"You can't, Mina."

Mina eyes flashed as she looked past me, and the sound of dry wings brushing against each other filled the room, and I went to her and pressed my lips against her forehead. Her pupils dilated, stretched so that the whites looked bruised, and I pulled away, felt the darkness inside of me singing to the darkness inside of her.

I stretched my body alongside hers, and she tucked her head against my chest, her hand over my heart, and closed her eyes. The television clicked off, and I smoothed my sister's hair, and sang to her, hoped that inside the glittering world the Dark Lady created she could follow my voice back to me.

Dad didn't speak when he came out of the kitchen but sat in the armchair next to us. His face was worn, as if I could lift it off with no effort and peer at all of the things he hid beneath. Mina twitched, and I pressed my skin to hers. "Don't listen to her," I whispered and hoped she heard me. Hoped that the pill she'd taken would tie her tongue and keep her from speaking. Keep her from saying the words I had been too afraid to.

"I didn't know what to do. After she died. Spent night after night staring at the ceiling and wondering how I was going to do it. I'm still not sure," Dad said, and I turned to him. He sat forward, his head leaned against his hands. "Every morning I'd wake up and want to ask her if I was doing it right, but her pillow would be cold, and I'd remember, and oh, God." His voice cracked, and he covered his face. I turned back to Mina and tried not to listen to Dad's sobs.

"When will she come back?" he said.

"Don't ask her to," I said, but I didn't think he could hear me. Mina smiled in her sleep, and my skin crept into gooseflesh. The television turned on again.

"They had hungry little mouths. Always crying in the middle of the night, and you couldn't sleep, and so you didn't dream, and eventually you forgot her face. Forgot the sound of her voice." The Dark Lady's voice crackled—a distorted, mechanical buzzing—and Dad turned to face the television, and his mouth went slack.

"There were nights they cried out for you, and you buried your head, covered your ears and pretended you didn't hear them, but they came scratching at your door, and so you went to them and wiped the tears from their faces and pressed cool washcloths to their foreheads and opened closet doors and lifted frilled bed skirts to check for monsters. You made sandwiches and braided their hair and stood behind them while they brushed their teeth, and every minute you thought of how much they looked like her. Like they'd sucked every bit of her into themselves, those greedy, little teeth open wide, and you wanted to break them open and pour them out and re-shape all the things you lost from their broken bones, like so many puzzle pieces spread across the ground."

A thin line of saliva worked its way down Dad's chin, and I looked away. The voice droned on, a lifted chorus of buzzing, mechanical voices, and Dad closed his eyes. The sound shouldn't have been beautiful. It was.

"Tell me what you want," the Dark Lady said, and then the world dropped away.

I COULD FEEL Mina next to me, her breath cold as she exhaled, and I shifted and pushed myself up. Dad was gone, and the house was dark.

"Mina. Wake up." I didn't try to hide the fear in my voice. If Mina had been with the Dark Lady, she would already know.

"He's gone. Isn't he?"

"Yes."

She opened her eyes. The whites were completely black now.

"What did you do, Mina? What the fuck did you do?" I wanted to scream at her, wanted to shake her until she was normal again, but my voice was a whisper, and she twitched her hands across my face.

"I gave him what he wanted. It won't last though. She told me. He'll wake up tomorrow and think it was a dream, and he'll wish his blood would freeze in his veins and his heart would stop. But he wanted it so much, Hayley. Wanted to see Momma again. Just for a moment." Her tears were as black as her eyes, and they stained her cheeks.

"He won't remember," I said, and she shook her head.

Mina took my hand, and together, we stood, walked through the kitchen, and opened the back door. We were both so hungry, and we went down on all fours, crept through the night's warm grass and found the skittering, squirming things and put them between our teeth and crunched down.

Mina sighed, and I went to her, and we traced our fingers over each other's faces. "Sister," she said, and I pressed my lips into her palm. "She gave us a new name." Mina reached under my shirt and traced the letters against my naked back, and I held the syllables in my mouth, too afraid to say them aloud.

"I don't want to say it either," Mina said, and I took her hand in mine, and we watched the moon and stars bleed into something else, something alien, and the earth broke open beneath us, the sound of wings fluttering and mandibles clicking as they opened and closed.

"Did she give Momma a new name, too?" I said, but I already knew the answer. We watched the sky and waited for the buzzing wings to melt into morning sun, but the night was long, and we shivered in our thin T-shirts and shorts.

"He'll come home. Won't he?" I said, and above us the sky came together and apart like the popped seams of a doll, and we pressed our bodies into the dirt as if we could take root, but there was nothing beneath us but emptiness.

When the sky finally began to change, we crawled back to the stairs. Went up, up, and up and pressed our faces to the window—our foreheads leaving a slick smear of oil against the glass—and stared inside the house.

"Do you see him?" Mina said.

"No. Not yet. But I can feel him breathing. Like the edges of it, you know? He's not completely back yet, but he's hiding somewhere. Behind everything. He'll be here soon," I said, and we opened the door. Our footprints dark smears against the linoleum and carpet, and we stretched ourselves on the couch like bookends, our toes barely touching.

"He'll ask for it again. If she comes back to him," I said.

"Probably."

"How much more will she ask for?"

"Whatever's left to give."

"And when there's nothing?"

Mina shrugged. Her eyes were back to normal, the deep brown surrounding the pinprick of her pupil.

From the hallway came the sound of someone shifting. A cold body coming awake.

"He came back," Mina said, and we turned our heads away. Neither of us wanted to see him, to see the blackened eyes that would surely be there.

The sun came through the blinds, lit the room and our prone bodies in gold, and we lay still as death, our eyes squeezed tight, tight, tight, until our father opened his door, and then he was past us, opening kitchen cabinets and muttering to himself.

Only when the thick smell of coffee floated through the air did we open our eyes, scrambled off the couch, and crawl back to our bedroom.

"Still hungry," Mina said. My own stomach clenched around emptiness, and I pressed my fingernails into the flesh there; the imprinted half-moons fading as quickly as they'd come.

"We'll have to wait."

"She already changed us. Didn't she? Without even asking."

"Yes."

Dad shuffled back down the hallway, and his bedroom door opened and closed, the lock clicking as he shut us out.

"How long do you think he'll be in there?" Mina's lids were already heavy, her voice drowsy and thick with sleep.

"Until he forgets. Until he knows it wasn't real." I said, but I knew he wouldn't forget. Would come back again and again to the memory, nudging it like a sore tooth, and he would try every night to slip back into the dream, and Mina and I would wither in our skins. It wouldn't ever change.

"I don't think I love him enough," Mina said. A cold thing to say, but I understood. She'd been too little when Momma died, and Daddy was already mostly gone, too.

We wrapped ourselves in our blankets and sat facing each other. I tried to memorize her face, but it was so much like looking into a mirror I found I could close my eyes and still see her, close as skin.

"Come and find me once we fall asleep, okay? She doesn't like it when you're there. In my dream. I don't think she likes it when we're together."

"Okay," I said, but I didn't know how to find her. Didn't know the way. When the sound began—the droning sound of wings taking flight—Mina tipped her head back but did not close her eyes.

"Sleep tight," she said. A giggle escaped her throat, but she didn't smile. She lay across the floor, the blanket tented over her head, and I reached across the space and wound my fingers through hers. I could taste her. Salt and sweet and, underneath everything, the slight tinge of putrefaction.

Legs and wings whirred against each other; phosphorescent skins gone transparent, and we tipped forward and looked with many eyes.

"I can take it out of you. Easy as anything. Pluck," the Dark Lady stood before me, her hands arched as if taking a ripe fruit from the vine. "Nothing at all really. And think of all the years unfolding before you. All for you."

My mouth opened, my teeth snapping for the soft, wet thing she held. "So hungry," I said and she smiled. There were no teeth to it. Only browned gums and a furred, slick tongue, and I covered my face.

"How long would it give me?" I said.

"Had we but world enough and time."

Somewhere back in the dim light of our bedroom, Mina's fingers pressed against mine. A tether holding me to her. To Dad. To the diseased things Momma passed to us.

My stomach ached, roared to be filled, and the Dark Lady brought that furred tongue to my cheek. "Is it enough, love? Could it ever be enough? And when your blood betrays you, your lungs mottled and diseased, will they be enough? Your father locked away in his bedroom dreaming of a dead woman. Your sister coughing secret blood into her palm and you pretending not to see. Your bodies fading into something you don't recognize, and your father standing over the three women he buried and then following them down into the dark." She lifted a lock of my hair off my shoulders. "Tell me what you want."

I opened my mouth. Swallowed.

"Please. I was the first," I said, and the light went out.

All That Is Refracted, Broken

Paul would only look at me through the mirror.

"This is the only way I can see your soul," he told me that last time, the time before he vanished, and he positioned the burnished bit of glass so that only my eyes were reflected. I blinked, and he angled the mirror beside my face, making sure I couldn't see inside, and counted my eyelashes aloud.

"Other people can look at me without a mirror. You don't need to see my soul to see me," I told him, but he shook his head, dark hair flying.

"Yes, I do. I have to be sure."

⬚

HE WASN'T SUPPOSED to live. Was supposed to drown inside Momma's belly, supposed to go to sleep and wink out like a star. When she told Daddy that the baby wouldn't survive, he said that he couldn't be with a woman who was broken and left us. Momma took all of our family pictures down. The empty hooks snagged at my sweaters whenever I walked past.

But then she came home with Paul clutched to her breast, a

squalling red thing, and he grew and laughed and spoke. But no matter how I cooed, how I sang, he wouldn't look at me, would duck his head and shift his eyes away any time I tried to catch his gaze.

Anyone, *everyone* else, he would stare at directly, green eyes unblinking and curious. It was only me, only his big sister, whose eyes he avoided. At first Momma said it was because he was just a baby, that he didn't know what he was looking at, but by his first, and then his second birthday, he still hadn't looked at me.

Momma took him to doctors, and words like *autism* and *Asperger's syndrome* floated through the house for months, but no diagnosis ever came.

"He's perfectly normal," the doctors told Momma.

"He talks to her. Plays with her like any other kid. He loves her. Why won't he look at her?"

"It's a phase. He'll grow out of it," they reassured her with soft voices, and I squirmed under their gaze. Surely they knew that it was me. That there was something wrong with *me* and that was why Paul would keep his head down whenever I entered the room, but they couldn't say it while I was there. When Momma was alone, they would explain that her girl was the problem.

My childish mind came back to the thought again and again. I had something inside of me that he didn't want to see. I prayed to God every night, promised him that I wouldn't complain when Momma made me scrub the toilet or eat rutabagas if only he would get rid of whatever it was lurking just under my skin.

Momma begged Paul. Told him she would buy him anything he wanted if he would just look at me, but he would always turn away. And my heart would break a little more.

⸺

BURIED under moth-eaten quilts and yellowed dishtowels, a

silvered glinting cast refracted light onto the ceiling, and Paul pulled the mirror out, polished it with his shirt.

"If you tilt it up and look down, it's like you're walking on the ceiling," I told him, and he did as I told him, took a few unsteady steps before tumbling forward, laughing the entire way down. I laughed with him.

I didn't understand then. I still don't. Not completely.

I'm not sure when he turned the mirror in my direction. There was only the gasp of surprise, the eruption of giggles, and his tiny fingers pressing into mine.

"I can see you!" he exclaimed, and I curled my hand around his and marveled at how love can make it hard to breathe. How the knowing of it is almost painful.

We spent the rest of the afternoon bent around one another, his fingers tracing the mirror. I told myself for a long time that I hadn't felt his touch against my skin, his childish hand poking my eyes, my nose. I told myself that I had imagined it, that we were only two children lost in the magic of a rain-dappled afternoon.

Seven years passed, his eyes watching me through only the mirror, and time swallowed the reality of that day.

I wish I had believed.

⸺

SOMETIMES HE DID THAT. Said that it was quieter down there, that he could sleep better. We would find him tangled in a nest of blankets, a pile of worn paperbacks stacked within arm's reach, a flashlight tucked under his arm.

But when I tiptoed downstairs, intent on scaring him awake, there were no blankets, no books, no gangly thirteen-year-old boy asleep on the floor. A part of me must have known something was wrong because my guts turned icy.

We searched the rest of the house, Momma saying over and over "He's here somewhere. He's got to be here somewhere."

But he was nowhere.

We called his friends from school, asked if he had turned up at their homes in the middle of the night, but each call led to nothing more than a mother who hung up the phone and went to check on her own children.

After that, Momma stopped talking.

When we had looked everywhere, asked everyone, I called the police.

Momma stared out the window while I spoke to them, described what he looked like, gave them his most recent school photo.

"We'll do all we can," they told us, but no amount of doing can bring back something that's vanished.

When they left, I screamed until my throat felt bloody. But it didn't bring him back.

⸻

"WHERE DID YOU GO?" I whisper to the emptiness of my bedroom.

I think I might drown in the silence of this house.

⸻

IT FELT HEAVIER than I remembered, and the backing was more tarnished, a deep layer of soot that would not wipe away.

He had never let me look into the mirror.

"It's only for me. You can't see your own soul. If you do, you'll go away and never come back," he'd told me not long after he found it.

"But you can see yourself in it, right?"

"It's different for me. I was supposed to die when I was a baby, so I can see things other people can't."

"Don't talk that way," I said.

But I'd humored him, and before long, I didn't think about

daring to peek. Perhaps I thought what he'd said was true. Perhaps I was afraid of what I might see, of what might happen.

MOMMA HASN'T MOVED in days. Won't eat. I don't know if she sleeps. She stares out the window, waiting for Paul.

If he comes home, he won't come through the front door.

"YEAH?"

He picked at his cuticles, fidgeted in his chair.

"Some people believe you can get your soul caught inside a mirror. That once it's there, it starts to go rotten. To get evil and stuff. Sometimes, the people don't even know their soul is in there, but when they die, they're stuck in the mirror, and they do terrible things to get out."

"Like what?"

"Like they trick people. And if they're strong enough, they can steal someone else's soul. Because that's what they want. More than anything. To get out of the mirror. To be human again. Most of the time when you look in the mirror, it looks just like you, but if you pay attention, you can see them moving around. And they watch us, too. Try to figure out ways to escape."

I turned to look at him then. He'd placed the mirror on the kitchen table. For the first time since he'd found it, it was face down, and he'd turned away from me.

"What kind of crap do they have in your library anyway?" I said.

I didn't think much of it then. Figured he'd seen a scary movie at a friend's house and had a few nightmares or read a few too many horror novels. It's what kids do.

But over the next few weeks, he followed me, the mirror

trained on my face, his step always behind me. Whenever I went to bed, he looked worried, and there were several nights I heard my bedroom door creak open, a mirrored flash landing against my eyes before the door would shut.

———

"PAUL? IS IT YOU?" I ask the mirror when it appears, but it doesn't respond.

I think Momma is dead, starved to death in her chair, but I'm afraid to look.

———

"I DON'T KNOW. I like it better this way. What if I did, and it wasn't you?"

"What do you mean? Of course it would be me. Who else would it be?"

He watched me through the mirror, his eyes dark.

"I don't know," he says again.

———

"WILL YOU COME BACK? Will you come back if I look?"

Light shines against the ceiling, shimmers and dances in ecstasy. I stand over the mirror, and I stare down, the ground dropping away from my feet.

The creature in the mirror isn't me. The eyes are all wrong, the cheeks too thin and hollow, the fingers long and crooked. The other me grins with broken teeth.

Then the image warps, bloats endlessly, and then the face is Paul's. He is pale, his lips gone white, but he smiles, and for the first time, his eyes look into mine, and all that remains of me shatters into tiny pieces.

I blink, and the reflection is just my own face again, and a slight shadow streaks into the corners.

"Oh, Paul," I say, and my reflection wraps its lips around my words, repeats them back to me soundlessly.

"What have you done?"

I can feel his hands on my face, his fingers wiping away the tears, and I press my own to the mirror, hope that in whatever nightmare world he's trapped himself to save us, he can feel my touch in the way that I can feel him.

But there's nothing more than the hard glass beneath my hands and a scream building in my belly.

Tonight, I will place the mirror under my pillow. Face up. If there is any magic left in the world, it will find the mirror there and bring my brother back. I swear I'll take his place.

Please. Let it bring him back.

December Skin

They'd found the motel just before dark. Big drips of sky painting the pines black and jagged, and the cold palpable and worming. They had not thought to bring jackets.

Rory crammed her meager body onto the floor of Aaron's old F100 while he fed lies to the rheumy-eyed manager. His pop was dying, and Aaron hadn't seen him in years. Divorce, you know? He was headed up there now, to pay his respects, get some things off of his chest before the old sonofabitch finally bit the big one. Couldn't he overlook that he was only seventeen and rent him a room, just for the night?

Pressing herself against the floor, Rory tried to absorb what residual heat she could from the engine. They'd been driving for hours now, outrunning the coming night, but the shadows had grown deep and full and Aaron had left her in the truck, the keys tucked deep into his right pocket. What she wanted was to sink those keys deep into his eye sockets, listen for the soft pop as the optic nerve separated. Her teeth chattered. From under the truck, something chattered back.

But there was the overhead light popping on, and Aaron

hauling himself behind the wheel. "Room's around back. We're going to have to run," he said and threw the truck into gear.

"You ever woken up in the middle of the night? You don't know why, but suddenly your just wide awake and staring at the ceiling, and you're sweating under the covers, and you're lying there, listening to your heart beat, and somehow, it just doesn't sound right? Like the beats are just slip-sliding around, and you take a couple of deep breaths. To regulate. Only it doesn't help, and for a few seconds, your heart just stops, and you can hear everything, all the silence that's in the spaces in between your heartbeats?"

"Don't," he said.

"You can fall into that space. Fall in and never climb out." From beneath the truck, the chattering grew louder.

"Stop it, Rory," he said, and she curled more tightly against the floorboard.

"You pretend, little brother. So full of your fake concern," she hissed, and she thought of touching him, letting him feel the coldness living in the place where her heart once beat, but he had to get her inside, had to get her away from the gathering night and even she knew this.

"Don't move. I'll come and get you," he said. Outside, over the truck's rumbling, something laughed deep and long.

When he cut the engine, he leaned against the steering wheel, let his hair fall over his face. Sitting that way, he looked like a child, small and tucked into himself. For a moment she wanted to reach out to him, but her hands twitched, and she smiled at the thought of ripping his scalp from skull.

Then he was moving, running through the gloom before throwing open the door and pulling her against him, her body suddenly weightless as he pulled her from the truck and shoved her toward a door.

The numbers glinted against the black. "1306! 1306!" they seemed to scream. One by one, the lights around them began to blink out, the doors of the other rooms disappearing, swallowed as if some rotting maw had opened and begun to eat.

She wanted to open her arms to it, whatever lurked beyond the world, wanted to breathe it in, hold it there in the cold places that filled her. Because she knew about them now, the things that lived on the periphery, in the spaces between. She would give herself to them, these eaters of skin, of innocence, and they would make of her something vast.

"Come on, come on!" Aaron said, and his fingers closed around the keys, fumbled once, twice, before slipping into the lock, and then they were tumbling into the room, Aaron slamming the door behind them before frantically throwing light switches.

A dull glow filled the small space. A single bed sat in the center, a yellowing quilt tucked military tight over the lumpy mattress. On the wall, a faded watercolor of cows grazing. Someone's idea of quaint, homey touches of Americana. A window opened to the exterior, spilled shadows into the room, and Aaron pulled the curtains closed. There was the deep, earthen smell of mold, and Rory breathed it in, letting the scent of decay spread through her lungs.

Aaron watched her now, the dark shadows under his eyes like bruises. He clenched his hands, both sets of keys bound tightly in his fists. If she looked at the light, tried not to think about what lurked outside the door, she could almost ignore the cold, could almost imagine that the thing that had crept inside of her was quiet. Something sleeping, but not dead.

He jerked his chin toward the bed. "You should get some sleep."

"Not tired. You're the one who should sleep. Driving like you have been."

He shook his head. *He doesn't trust you*, she thought. It made her smile to know this. He had more sense that she'd ever given him credit for. Where she was the intellectual, the literary-minded obsessive who quoted Joyce and Rand, Aaron was a video game addict whose Neolithic grunting only stumbled into actual speech when ordering at Taco Bell.

"Is it better," he said. A statement rather than a question.

"In the light? You know it is."

"But it isn't gone. It's still in there. Waiting for it to get dark."

She had no response for him, and he turned his head away, stared at the window. It had been Aaron who found her with the cat, huddled in the shadows of the porch as she ate sloppily, slimy strings of meat stuck in her teeth.

"The fuck," he'd said, and she'd grinned at him, her eyes yellow bright in the darkness.

He'd taken her inside, wiped the blood from her face, her arms and fingers before putting her to bed, but she hadn't slept. Instead, she'd whispered to him, told him about the deep emptiness between the beats of a heart, told him that they had found her there at the bottom of that hole and filled her up with cold and night. He'd stayed with her, listened quietly as she told him of darkness.

Two weeks later, she woke under the porch, her skin sticky and streaked with mud and crimson. Before her lay a tiny frilled dress, the light pink mottled with darker stains. She'd asked him to take her away then, asked if he could keep her from the dark. If he would run with her, keep her from doing this thing to the people they loved. And he had.

Outside of the window, something scratched, the high-pitched hum of claws against glass. When Aaron turned two middle fingers in the direction of the sound, Rory laughed. It felt good to laugh, to push all of the cold somewhere else for the briefest of moments.

"Fuck you, motherfuckers!" she screamed, and Aaron pumped his fingers toward the window before leaping on the bed, jumping up and down.

"Fuck you!" Aaron threw back his head and screamed, a raw, bloodied howl that sounded more animal than human. The exhaustion, the anger, the fear all poured into this single sound. Once, it would have set her nerves on edge. Now, the cold that lived inside of her stirred—a sleek, velvet movement—and she licked her lips.

Night had completely fallen. She could feel it moving inside of her, the cold barely contained by the scant light of the room. Hungry. Searching. Daylight was better. It moved easily in the dark, slipping among the shadowed places where people either didn't or were too afraid to look. Rory had looked too long. She always had. There was too much space in her head, too much silence and stillness to lose herself in. Maybe that was why she had filled it with books, complex ideas that filled the emptiness. It was always in the night, in the quiet that she lost the thread that tethered her to this world. Whatever *it* was, it had seen her, felt her. All that void asking to be filled.

Aaron sat down on the edge of the bed, his fingers clenched around the quilt. Dirty fingernails digging against the thin material.

"You can feel it now. Inside," he said, and she nodded.

She moved across the room, sat beside him, and he flinched at the closeness. The desire to scramble away from her, to hurl himself across the room was tangible, a raw, bleeding thing suspended between the two of them. She could feel it. But he stayed, reached a hand across the quilt to grasp hers, and she squeezed his fingers. He was real, the living, breathing thing that connected her to this world, and he would help her fight.

"I miss Mom," he said.

"Me too," she said. He dropped her hand then, the warmth of his fingers suddenly absent, and she hated the cold that flooded through her, always probing, always searching.

"If we hadn't left, do you think you would have …"

"No," she said, but he glanced up at her, his eyes unblinking, and they both knew that what she had spoken was a lie. She hated herself a little bit more.

"I don't know, Aaron," she whispered, and he nodded.

"I'm fighting. So hard. But I lose myself. It's like falling into a hole, only you can't see the bottom. There's just cold and dark, and the edges of the world bleed away, and all that's left is that *thing* peeling you open, eating its way into you," she said.

"You read too many books, nerd," he said and smiled. It was a small, broken thing, but she loved him for it.

A cold wind howled, and the lamps flickered, blinked out once, twice.

In the quick flashes of dark, Rory saw Aaron sprawled before her, his skin peeled open, a wide, grinning mouth carved against his stomach. Once more, her tongue darted across her lips, and the cold gathered just beneath her skin. *Sleeping, but not dead.*

"No," she said through clenched teeth. Not here. Not now. Under flesh and bone, the thing stirred, but she pushed it away, willed it to sleep, to be silent.

"What?" Aaron said, but she shook her head.

"Nothing. It's nothing," she said. He stood then, walked to the door, placed his palm flat against it.

"Do you remember when we were kids, and you used to get so mad because I'd sneak in your room at night if I got scared?" he said.

"You wet the bed a couple of times. I'd have a dream that I was swimming and wake up with piss up to my neck."

"But you never kicked me out," he said and turned to her. Again she saw him as a child, like the boy he had been. Once, she had protected him from the things hiding in the dark. She wished she still could.

"We should sleep," he said.

"Yeah. I'll take the floor," she said and grabbed a pillow.

"It's okay," he said.

"No, Aaron," she said, but he came back to her, placed a firm hand on her shoulder.

"It's okay, Rory."

He waited as she curled her body against his as she had

when they were nightmare-plagued children. She watched the light as his breath grew longer, heavier. It did not flicker but blazed out strong and resolute. She smiled into her brother's shoulder. And she slept.

There was no light when she woke. Only the cold creeping throughout the room and all of those hidden spaces opening like little mouths stretched wide. She stood, opened the door, the window. Behind her, Aaron did not move.

Split Tongues

The dreams start up the week after my father spoke in tongues for the first time.

Mom doesn't like it that he takes me to church, but she isn't there to nag at him anymore, not since the divorce papers finally came through, and so I drag my happy ass out of bed every other Sunday and straighten my hair so that he can cart us to the His Holiness Church of New Hope.

I don't mind it that much. It's boring, don't get me wrong, but Alec Mitchell sits in the third pew, and my dad sits in the fourth, so I pass the service mouthing the hymns and wondering what it would be like trace my tongue along the hard line of his jaw or to tug my fingers through that shock of black hair and kiss him long and hard.

Alec never turns around, and he never notices me standing there in the pew at the end of the service, my fingers tugging at the scooped collar of my dress so that he can see that I actually have some cleavage. Once I thought he would at least smile at me, but his mother called to him, and he hurried past without even looking up.

Pastor Fuller smiles at me every time he sees me. "Sister

Brianne," he says, and I don't like the sound of my name in his mouth or the way he touches me, the bony fingers massaging my shoulder. It makes me feel like an insect caught in a web.

Still every other weekend, Dad comes to pick me up, and I spend Saturday pretending to listen to him pray and read his verses from the Bible while tears stream down his cheeks. I almost feel sorry for him, but then I remember the afternoon that I came home and found him on the couch with Kelley Browning—who was on the cheerleading squad with me—his face buried against her crotch.

Kelley was already eighteen, so no one could press any charges, but Mom threw all of Dad's shit out onto the lawn, and it didn't matter how much he begged or hollered that he'd found Jesus because Mom was done with his bullshit, and now he has partial custody. At least until I'm eighteen. Six more months, and I'm out of this hell hole forever.

Alec Mitchell doesn't notice me in school either, and I pretend that I'm not looking at him in AP Lit. The teacher doesn't give a shit what we do, so I just put in my ear buds and watch him out of the corner of my eye.

He has this way of licking his lips while he's reading. Like a nervous tic, but he doesn't have a reason to be nervous, and I imagine what it would be like to bite at his lower lip, to draw it into my mouth. He's probably never even kissed anyone before, and more than anything, I want to be his first.

In the dark quiet of the sanctuary, with dust and dead prayers in my lungs, I want to kiss him. I want to make him forget that he's supposed to think it's wrong. Make him forget that he's supposed to save himself for some pure, beautiful girl who doesn't exist. I want to be the thing that guides him forward into the shadows, and I want him to open his mouth and say yes.

I watch him and doodle in my notebook and think about the dream. Ever since Dad stood up in the middle of a service, his eyes rolled back so that only the whites showed, a garbled yammering streaming out him while he swayed, unsteady on his feet, the dream comes every night.

I'm always in the church, but it isn't the church, not really, and I'm alone, and it's dark. There is something caught in my throat, and I choke on it, gag as I try to bring it up, and something dark and viscous dribbles from my mouth and stains the white dress that I'm wearing.

I wake up, and I can't breathe, and it feels like there is something sitting on my chest, something with transparent lips pressed to my neck before a tongue I cannot see circles my nipple, and I think of Alec until it feels like all the air in the room hasn't been sucked out.

"Brianne?" Ms. Yardley stands over me, her face a mask of concern, and I sit up. "The bell rang."

"Right. Sorry," I mumble and gather my things and hurry out of the classroom. Thank God it's Friday and the last class of the day, or I'd be in some major shit with Mom. One more unexcused tardy, and no graduation trip to Cancun.

The hallways are already empty, and I pull my keys out of my purse and check my phone. No messages. Figures. Ever since Dad's little escapade, no one talks to me.

"You're Brianne, right?" The voice is soft. A voice I've heard only once or twice in class but imagined saying my name more times than I can count.

"Yeah," I say and look up at Alec. His eyes are the color of wet moss, and there are dark circles beneath them, but he is beautiful, and I try to think of something else to say, something to ask him, anything to keep him standing in front of me.

When he brings his lips to my ear, I freeze. He smells of cinnamon and something older. Something rotted. Like a pool of rainwater clotted with dead leaves.

"You're having the dream, too. Aren't you?" he whispers. My throat clicks when I swallow, but he doesn't wait for me to respond and before I can open my mouth, he's gone.

I drive home with his smell on my skin. My mother

complains when I tell her that I want to go to Dad's this weekend, but she doesn't tell me that I can't.

"I'll never understand how you can stand to even be around him. Not after …" she says, and I shrug my shoulders and drag my fork through the salad she made us for dinner. She's trying to find a new boyfriend, and so it's salads and chicken breast with no oil and steamed vegetables all of the damn time.

I don't want to tell her that he's different now. Quieter. I don't want to tell her about his Bible verses or how I can hear him in the middle of the night speaking in tongues, the words leaking out of him like blood. I don't want to tell her how the small sound of his words makes me afraid or how I think that if I rose and walked down the hallway to his room, he would be gone. The only thing left of him that voice spewing nothing into the room.

That night, the dream is different. Alec sits in his pew, and I can see the back of his head, his hair like raven's feathers. I try to call to him, but more of that dark liquid dribbles from between my lips, and I choke, the words a tangled mess.

It sounds like I am speaking in tongues.

When I wake up in the morning, my sheets are gone. I search the room but can't find them.

I don't eat breakfast, and Mom doesn't say anything because she's too busy swiping right or some dumb shit on her phone to notice.

"Did you call your father?" she says, not looking up.

"I texted him. He'll be here at ten. I'll just leave my car here."

"Fine," she says and stands and brushes a stray lock of hair from her face. After the divorce, she dyed it platinum and cut it short. Like Jamie Lee Curtis without the bone structure to make it work. Whatever. As long as she's happy, I guess.

"Did you take my sheets?"

"What?"

"My sheets. To wash them or something. Did you take them?" I say, and she stares back at me.

"No. You're old enough to wash your own sheets, Brianne," she says, and then she is gone.

Dad picks me up right at ten, and we don't speak as the roads bleed past in a haze of dull, monotone color. Everything is painted in Georgia December drab. I think of the acceptance letter to the University of Michigan that I haven't shown Mom or Dad. I want to see snow, want to see and feel more than this *nothingness* that I understand better than the feeling of my own skin wrapped around this miserable cage of bones.

The drive goes on and on, and I lean my head against the cool window and think about Alec and the dream and the way his whisper settled somewhere deep in my stomach. I think about how this Sunday will be different than all of the other Sundays, and I think of my father kneeling at the altar, his voice lifted high and quaking over all of the other voices as he speaks in tongues.

Dad doesn't talk to me for the rest of the afternoon, and that's fine by me. He doesn't have a TV—says that it's a portal to the world of sin—so I doodle in my notebook and ignore the silence of my cellphone. Mom texts me around five, but it's just to say that she's going out that night, and that she'll see me tomorrow afternoon and to be sure to finish whatever home-work I have. I go back to my notebook.

Ink stains my fingertips, and I trace my pen over the page again and again. The marks dip and converge, a bloated series of lines that intersect haphazardly and then zoom off again before curling into themselves.

My hand is tired, so I stop and crack my knuckles one by one. The pinkies and the thumbs, too. Dad locked himself in his bedroom the minute we came home. Praying or reading his Bible, I guess.

When everything first happened, he tried to talk to me. Tried to apologize and cried and snotted all over while he told me how sorry he was, that he'd just been so unhappy, that he was sick of himself and would never do anything like that again. Once he found Jesus, he stopped apologizing.

He doesn't come out of his room that night, and I heat myself up a can of tomato soup and check my phone again. Nothing.

"Dad?" I say and knock on his door. I can hear him murmuring, hurried whispers seeping out of the bottom of the door, but he doesn't respond, so I flip the closed door the bird and walk back to the second bedroom he keeps for me. An air mattress with a thin blanket lies on the floor, and I flop onto it, my ribcage grazing the hardwood beneath. Dad didn't inflate it all the way, and I have no idea where the pump is, so I grab the blanket and head back out into the living room to sleep on the sofa.

The sofa is lumpy in all of the wrong places, but in minutes I know that I'm asleep because I'm in the dream. My throat clogs with the thing I cannot see, and I gag and choke, but nothing comes up.

"Open your mouth," the voice comes from my right. Alec's voice, but I can't see him. "Open your mouth," he says again, and then his fingers tap against my teeth, and I swallow them down, and they are long and smooth and taste of strawberries.

He pulls and tugs and then the thing is sliding from my throat and falls with a wet plop against my lap. I still can't see Alec, but I look down at the thing staining my dress.

It's a piece of my tongue.

━━━

HE GRABS HIS KEYS, and I follow him outside where the air tastes of ice, but there is only rain.

"Dad," I start, and he turns to me, but I don't finish. I'm not even sure what I wanted to say. Mom thinks I should be angry at him, but every time I look at him all of the anger I've stored up leaks out of me, and I just feel sorry for him.

We turn off of the highway and onto the gravel road that leads to the church. It's a small building, tucked away behind a curving drive lined with cypress trees.

He cuts the engine but doesn't open his door; he just sits and looks out at the trees, and his skin looks as if its soaked in all of the pale morning light, and I realize that he's going to die one day. This man who used to hold the back of my bicycle until I learned to push the pedals on my own. This man who checked under my bed and inside of my closet when there were monsters that needed chasing away.

When he turns to face me, his eyes glint, and for a moment, I think that I see a different color, not the deep blue I've always known, but a bleached out gray, and he blinks, and everything is as I've always known it. "I'm sorry, Brianne," he says, and then he is opening his door, and the air swirls into the car and lifts my hair, and I am alone.

Through the window I watch him walk into the church, his shoulders lifted and straight, nothing at all like the hunched man who used to haunt the rooms of our old house.

The heavy wood door opens, and my father passes through into the dim vestibule. In those suspended seconds, as my eyes focus and re-focus on the shadows that flit through the space, I see Alec standing just beyond the door, and he is watching me, and his hands are open.

I get out of the car. Cocooned inside of the winter air and white sky, I count the spaces between my heartbeats.

I go into the church.

━━━

ALEC HAS SPENT the service next to his mother, his face trained on Pastor Fuller as he rained down spittle and God's judgment, but now, as Pastor Fuller leans against my father, Alec turns to me, and he looks at me.

The voices of the congregation rise, their tongues spilling words intended for their God, and I think that the sound will break the world wide open.

No one notices when I begin to choke. No one notices when I cough the wriggling pink bit of flesh into my hand. No one notices when I run.

Behind me, Alec's voice strains and breaks high and clear above everyone's. It sounds like a scream.

In the restroom, I wrap the bit of tongue in toilet paper and flush it. Sweat beads against my lower back and between my thighs, and I breathe through my mouth and tell myself that I'm not going to be sick.

When the door opens, I go still, hold my breath so that I can listen for footsteps, and I pull myself onto the toilet and draw up my feet.

The sound that comes from outside the stall door is the clattering of hard nails against the tiled floor. It's the sound of an animal creeping.

Beneath the door, there are no feet, no high-heeled shoes that could be the sound, no claws, but the sound still comes, and I close my eyes tight, tight, tight and push my face into my shoulder and bite at the muscle there so that I won't scream.

Outside of the door, the sound pauses, and the lock shakes, and I whimper. "Please," I say, but the lock slides back, and the door opens, and all I can do is swallow my tears.

"You okay, sweetie?" An older woman dressed in a denim jumper, her hair piled atop her head in an elaborate braided bun stands in front of me. Her lips cave in on her mouth, and I realize that she has no teeth.

My heart is in my throat, and I cannot speak. She comes into the stall with me and pats my back. I don't want her there, want to tell her to get the fuck out, but everything I want to speak is buried inside of me, and so I sob and let her push my hair out of my face and hand me tissue after tissue.

Inside of my throat, something fleshy scrapes and pokes at the lining there, and I choke, and she hands me another tissue, and I cough and cough until another bit of tongue tumbles out. I tuck the tiny piece of me into my fist, and the older lady rubs my back until I quiet, and then she smiles at me and asks if I'll be okay.

"Yes," I say, and she stands, her large hips bumping against the stall door as she leaves.

I ball the tissue up and put it in my pocket. When I go to sleep tonight, perhaps I will place that bit of tongue beneath my pillow. Perhaps the dream will change. Perhaps it won't.

The vestibule is empty when I leave the restroom. Everyone is still inside of the sanctuary, still shouting those terrible words into the sky, and I want to throw open the doors. "You aren't saying *anything*. It means *nothing*," I want to scream at them, but the door on the far left opens just a crack, just enough to let a sliver of light leak into the gloom.

Alec slips through, and I think I see him shimmer, his arms and legs thin as smoke and then they are solid again, and he turns to face me and holds out his hand. "Can I see it?" he says.

My fingers spider over the small, wet bit in my pocket. I don't want to give it to him. It came from me. It's mine.

"No," I tell him, and he drops his hand and nods. The air is thick and sluggish, and I need out of this room, out of this church. When I go, Alec follows me.

I walk into the trees until all I can see is green. No bright sky, only the color of new things drowning out the world, and then Alec is behind me, and I am speaking to him in words that I don't understand but I do understand, and his eyes are darker now, the color of a black moth, and he tells me about the dream. How it's the same as mine. How he's had it for as long as he can remember. How he used to believe, but now, he doesn't. He can't.

"It isn't God they are talking to. It isn't," he says, and I understand.

When I kiss him, he doesn't touch me, doesn't run his hands through my hair or over my collarbone, but he traces his tongue over mine, and I press against him. He is hard in the way that the other boys have been, but I don't tug at his zipper, don't move my hand over that soft flesh in the way that I have before. Other boys with their insistent hands and their loud groaning that it isn't right to get them so worked up, and can't I just? Just a little? And I always did because I didn't want the silence that has still somehow found me, this silence that my father laid at my feet like a jewel.

But Alec doesn't push against the back of my head or guide my hands further and further down. He only kisses me and bites at my lips, and there is the ancient taste of blood in my mouth.

"Don't," I say when he pulls away. I keep my eyes closed and reach for him, but there is only the air, and I open my eyes.

I am alone.

One foot in front of the other, I walk back to the car where my father waits behind the wheel. Something different curls inside of his skin. Something that is not my father ruffles my hair and asks me in a voice older than the earth if I feel okay.

I know these things because I tasted them on Alec's tongue.

"Take me home," I say to the thing that is not my father, and he smiles a smile that has too many teeth. I won't look at that smile. I refuse.

Mom stops me when I come through the door. Her hands are feather light on my shoulders, and she grasps at my coat so that I can't sneak past her and up to my room.

"Are you sick?" she asks.

"No."

"I swear, Brianne, if you're sick and that asshole didn't take you to the doctor."

"I'm not sick, Mom. Just tired."

She unclenches the fabric bound in her fingers, but she

leaves her hands on my shoulders. "I wish you wouldn't go over there."

"I have to."

"No." She shakes her head. "You don't."

"Mom. I just want to go to bed. Okay?"

"How …" She pauses and licks her lips. There is a sore in the right corner. "How do you not hate him?"

"I don't know," I tell her, and it's the truth. "Please. I'm tired."

She lets me go, and I don't look back at her. In my bedroom, I pull the piece of tongue from my pocket. It feels larger in my palm. Heavier. I don't unwrap it but place it under my pillow and curl on top of it like a cat. My room is too warm, but I'm too exhausted to get up and turn on the fan.

Underneath my pillow, the tongue whispers.

I don't sleep.

———

I WANT to call her a bitch. I want to call her a whore and to grab her by the hair and drag her through the hallway until the strands rip away from her scalp.

Instead, I do nothing, and she walks away and laughs at me with the bitch group of friends she has who were once my friends, too.

In sixth period, Alec is absent, and I spend the hour staring at his empty desk. I trace the spots where his body should be, the places where I touched him only the day before.

Mom isn't home when I let myself into the house, but there is someone upstairs. Footsteps that pause and then start up again and the sound of something breathing.

"Brianne?" a voice calls down to me, and it's Alec's voice.

"How did you get in here?" I ask him when I open my bedroom door. He's lying on my bed, his head pressed against the pillow, dark hair feathered out across the white fabric, and he has his eyes closed tight, tight, tight. Scrunched up so that he looks like he doesn't have eyes at all, only eyebrows, and I sit on the bed next to him.

"I woke up here. Went to sleep and then I was here." He opens his eyes and brings his fingers to my lips. They taste of salt.

He tucks his hands underneath my pillow, and he looks so young. Like a little boy waiting for his mother to come and kiss him goodnight. A little boy who should be frightened of the dark or of monsters in the closet.

"I kept them everywhere when they first came. In my drawers. Under my mattress. I buried them next. Everywhere in my backyard are little graves. But it doesn't matter. The dreams come anyway."

I crawl into bed with him, and he wraps his body around me, and he is warm, and I am cold, and I squeeze my eyes shut as tight as his were.

Underneath my pillow, the tongue whispers, and we listen.

When the time comes, we answer.

━━━

I DON'T LIFT my pillow to check and see if the tongue—*my* tongue—has grown in the night. Instead, I go downstairs. Mom still isn't home. Must have found someone interesting on the little app she's always staring at.

I could stay home. Mom isn't there to keep me from skipping. I could sit on the couch all day and watch terrible daytime television and raid the refrigerator and maybe even steal one of the bottles of vodka Mom keeps in the freezer and get drunk off of my ass.

But the tongue is upstairs, and I can hear the dark stain of its whispers, and so I grab my keys and drive to school.

I'm early. The doors aren't even open yet, and so I head

back to the car, let the engine idle and turn the heat up so that it streams over my hands.

I don't remember leaning the seat back or closing my eyes, but when I open them the light coming through the window is the softer shade of afternoon sun, and I bolt upright. The clock on the dash reads 4:45, and the parking lot is as empty as it was this morning.

Grabbing my phone, I pull up the text messages. Three from my mother. All telling me that she got a call from the school and that my ass had better have a good excuse because life as I know it is over.

I try to turn the engine over, but the car sputters, and I look down at the gauges. Out of gas. Of course.

I'm not looking at the parking lot but looking beyond it, trying to figure out what the hell I should do, when I see it. Something dark moving along the ground. At first, I think it's a stray dog or cat, but the closer it gets, I realize that it's too large to be an animal, and it isn't moving the way that animals do.

It's jerky and stiff-legged and crawls on all fours as if it isn't used to the skin that wraps it. As if it wants to outrun whatever holds it all together.

And then it is close enough to see, and it is a man creeping along the ground. A man with long, tapered fingers covered with dirt, and he looks up at me, and I know his eyes, know the bend of his smile, know the sound of his voice.

"Dad," I say, and the sound echoes back to me all hollow. Like I've been emptied out. Like there is nothing at all left inside of me.

He stares at me—his eyes a dark smear—and his mouth twists, words pouring out of him like water, his tongue bending around strange syllables, and I can hear him even though I shouldn't be able to.

Then he is gone, loping off again into the woods that line the parking lot, and I'm shaking and crying too hard to even pick up my phone, but finally, I do.

"Mom," I say when she picks up, and I hear her sharp intake of breath. "Come get me. Please come and get me."

"Brianne? Are you hurt? Did someone hurt you?"

"No," I say, and my fingers fumble with the automatic locks, and I wait for the click, but none comes. I'll have to do it myself —one by one—but I can't move. Can't breathe.

"Where are you? I'm coming. Right now," she says, and I choke and I gag, and I don't look when that bit of tongue comes up.

"Please. The school," I say, and then I cannot speak.

━━━

I KEEP WATCHING the tree line, keep waiting for my father to re-appear, his body rushing along the ground and his mouth spilling words of holy fire.

"Open the door," my mother says over and over. A prayer. A litany for the dead.

When I do, she pulls me out of the car and into her arms, but I don't feel safe. I watch the tree line.

"Let's go, sweetie," she says, and I let her put me into her car. She drives, and I try not to think of the feeling of my tongue in my throat. "Brianne, you have to tell me what happened. Okay? You have to tell me."

"I fell asleep. I had a bad dream," I say, and she pulls the car over to the shoulder.

"If someone hurt you, I swear to fucking Christ ..."

"No." It's all that I can give her.

She looks at me, and her mouth is drawn up into a hard line. "I'm taking you to the emergency room."

I don't fight her or tell her that I'm fine. That I saw something I couldn't have possibly seen, heard something that wasn't there.

When the doctor comes into the room, he and Mom talk,

and I catch a few words here and there. Trauma. Catatonic. Shock.

The doctor is old enough to fart dust, and he is talking to me, but it's like I'm deep, deep underwater, and his words are bloated, fleshy things. "An exam. Just to be sure. It won't hurt at all," he says, and I nod.

When the nurse comes in, she smiles at me with a mouth frosted in baby pink, and she asks me what happened, tells me that if it's okay, they need for me to take everything off so they can be sure I'm not hurt.

I do what they ask me. I lift my arms and my legs and let them look at the smooth, unbroken skin, and I let them swab between my legs, and I whisper over and over, "Nothing happened."

But it's a lie because I squeeze my eyes shut, and the tiny hospital room disappears, and I see my father crawling along the ground like a spider as he speaks the language of his God, and I am afraid.

"Brianne? I'm going to look inside of your mouth now. Is that okay?" the nurse asks.

I open my mouth. She presses against my tongue and looks. Whatever she's searching for isn't there, and so she sighs and pats my shoulder. Tells me that I'm a good girl and that I've done very well.

My mother sits in a straight-backed leather chair in the far corner and watches the nurse and the doctor flutter around me. She doesn't move except to pick at her sweater.

Two hours later, the doctor is satisfied, and they send me home, tell my mother that I may be overtired. That I need rest and liquids. "There's nothing wrong with her," they say and give me a prescription for a sleeping pill and the phone number for a therapist. Mom thanks them, and she takes me home.

"We'll talk in the morning," Mom says after she's watched me take the sleeping pill; after she's pulled my sheets against my chin. She pauses, and I think she's going to kiss me. The way she used to when I was little. The way she used to when Dad was still here. But she's gone, and I'm alone, and everywhere is dark.

The tongue isn't under my pillow anymore, and I run my hands against the cool, empty space. I close my eyes.

It doesn't take long for the whispers to start up. The pill has left me woozy, but I manage to sit up. Propped against my pillow, I listen for my father's prayers, for him to speak in tongues.

"Brianne," he says, and his voice comes from beneath me.

He's under my bed. I picture him lying there, his back pressed into the floor and dust on his cheeks.

"I'm so tired, Dad."

He is speaking now, the words tumbling one after the other, and I am the only one to hear him.

When I finally fall asleep, my father's voice leaks into my dreams. I sit on our church pew, and bits of my tongue fall from my lips, and I cannot wake. I cannot.

Alec is there. He holds my hand and watches as I choke up piece after piece of myself.

"This is my body," he says, and he opens his mouth, places my tongue inside of his teeth. "This is my blood."

He swallows me down, and I curl inside of him, wrap myself in his warmth, and his lips are on mine, and he feeds me. I drink him down, and it's like drinking the sky, like taking the stars inside of myself, and he burns everything away.

"Who are they talking to?" I ask him, and he brushes my hair back from my face.

"I don't know," he says, and I shiver. It's winter inside of the church, and the white dress I wear is so thin.

"Why is this happening?"

"Does it matter?"

"No," I say, and then his teeth are on my neck, and his hands are on me, and all around us come the voices as they speak in tongues.

When he presses himself into the cleft between my legs, I

open my mouth and the tongues spill out of me. Beautiful and terrible, the sound beats against us with the strength of many wings, and we bend beneath it. We stretch and break, and the sound fills up all of the broken pieces, and we come together and come apart, sparking like shards of flint. Our cheeks are wet. I'm not sure if it's with tears or blood.

Somewhere in my bedroom, my father creeps in the dark. His words spill into the shadows, and I think that I must be drowning inside of them.

Alec pulls back and looks down as he moves above me. All around is my father's voice. Shadows steal through the church as if some great hole has opened and all of the things that move in the world beyond have come through. Things we aren't supposed to see.

"Is that what they pray to?" I say and point, but Alec does not turn to look.

"I've always known them," he says. "It's no use looking."

I try to watch for the shadows, but they slip away, and Alec's body is pumping against me, and it is too much to bear, this feeling. Everything inside of me is ripping apart, and my back arches, and there is a sweetness in the back of my throat as he brings his mouth to mine. It is something like sugar, something like honey, when I bite down on his tongue.

It is something beautiful when it splits in my throat. A tiny seed taking root.

A lovely thing to spill from between my lips in words that only Alec and I can understand.

We will whisper our love in tongues of fire.

"Yes," I open my mouth and tell them.

"Yes."

To Sleep in the Dust of the Earth

Lea and I met Beth when we were thirteen. That was the year Lea had legs that wouldn't fill out her shorts. The year I started sneaking Marlboro Lights from my mother's purse to share with Lea in the back corner of Benjamin Harper's abandoned lot.

"He was going to build on it. A house for his wife. But she died, and he just ..." Lea made a fluttering motion with her fingers, scattered the smoke streaming from her lips.

"Jesus. We've only heard the story about a million times. Give it a rest."

"I just think it's sad is all. You don't have to be such a bitch about it, Willa," Lea said and flicked her butt into the grass.

There were rumors that the lot was haunted. Little kids would dare each other to sneak out there at night. Sit right where the front door should have gone and stay until morning. For the older kids, it was place to do all of the things our parents said we shouldn't. Even still, we hung at the periphery of the land, far from the heart of the house Harper would have built.

"You don't feel something when we come out here? It's so quiet. My hair gets all prickly," Lea said.

"Like something big is about to happen. Like right before a

door opens. When you don't know who's on the other side." She looked somewhere just over my shoulder.

"Someone's here," she said and let out a deep groan. Her eyes fluttered into her skull, and she began to twitch, her fingers going rigid, and her back arching.

"Stop it," I said, and she let out two more guttural grunts before dissolving into giggles.

"Seriously, Lea. It's not fucking funny," I said and pushed her. She tumbled backward, and then, for what couldn't have been more than two maybe three seconds, I couldn't see her. Dark hair and eyes caught in the act of falling suddenly vanished among grass grown tall.

Must have been a trick of the afternoon sunlight because there she was again, those legs in the dirt and a smile streaked across her face.

"You asked for it," she said and brushed her hands over her thighs. "Shit. SHIT. Godammit, Willa," she said, her fingers spread wide.

"Nope. Not falling for it again."

"No. My ring. My *mom's* aquamarine ring. It's gone. She'll kill me."

"It must have fallen off when you fell. Hold on. We'll find it."

Later, Lea and I would chew Klonopin and tell each other that there was nothing strange about the day Beth stumbled into our lives. We were just two girls kneeling in the grass, hands outstretched. We must have felt her. Positions of supplication. Must have noticed the moment the sky went darker and the birds fell silent. I don't think we ever got up from that place. Not really. I think there will always be the two of us seeking something that will not be found.

"There's a hole here." Lea said, and I peered over her shoulder.

"Looks like an animal den or something."

"I think I see it," she said and poked her fingers into the entrance.

"Don't just shove your hand in there! It could be a snake hole. Don't you pay any attention in school?"

"Doesn't matter any way. Hand's too big. Help me find something to hook it. A long stick."

We have different memories of the first time we heard Beth's voice. For me, Beth sounded like someone trying very hard to not be heard. A quiet rush of words that she hoped would fall from her lips and into the dirt. Lea said that Beth's voice sounded like water. Something that slipped into your head and sloshed around so that you couldn't get it out no matter how hard you tried.

"I can get your ring for you." Beth looked whitewashed. Skin the color of oatmeal. A beige jumper that brushed a pair of knobby knees over a white T-shirt and a pair of crummy, knock off Keds. The kind of girl you see but don't spend too long looking at.

Lea turned to me and rolled her eyes. "I can't deal with this weirdo right now. My mother is going to hit the fucking roof. I'm not even supposed to touch the damn thing."

"I don't think we need your help," I said and turned my back to her. Message sent loud and clear.

"I'm Beth. I just moved here," she said, and Lea muttered something under her breath about being a homing beacon for idiots.

"Really. I can," Beth said and pushed her way between us.

"Is she fucking serious?" Lea said, but Beth only smiled and thrust her hand inside the hole.

"No way your hand is that small," Lea said.

"Maybe she has baby hands or something," I said.

Even now, I wonder if it was the lot acting on Beth. Leaking into her like venom into blood. Most of the time, I think that it was Beth all along. That the darkness we came to know was already a part of her. That she released herself into that place. Into us.

I think I'm still choking on her.

When Beth handed the ring to Lea, the gem cast glittering flecks across Lea's cheeks. She stood before us, head bowed, while Lea stuck the ring in her mouth to suck off the grit.

"Thanks. Really. You have no idea the shit storm that was coming my way. Your hands must be fucking tiny," Lea said once the ring was safely back on her finger.

"I'm Beth," she said again.

We should have never told her our names. Sometimes, things are meant to be lost. There are things you aren't supposed to go looking for.

Sometimes, it doesn't matter.

———

ALWAYS, Beth was in the background. Hovering behind us while we tested the waters of adulthood. Always watching with her quiet, pale smile. For four years she'd been with us. We didn't tell her to leave.

Even after all that time, we didn't know much about her. She didn't answer most of our questions when we asked them. There were the things that she told us: that her father moved the two of them here after her mother died; that he stood outside of her bedroom at night—to be sure she was breathing; that her favorite color was yellow. Sunshine yellow. The color of joy.

There were the things that she did not tell us: why we weren't allowed to come into her house; why she never spoke of her father after the first time she told us about him; why we never saw him—not at school to pick her up, not at the grocery store, not at PTSA meetings or driving his car or the hundreds of other ways you'll see someone's father; why she had scratch marks on the inside of her thighs.

Eventually, we stopped asking questions, and Beth faded into the background of our lives until we needed her.

During those four years, Beth found all of the things we lost: my favorite lipstick that I thought was in the bottom of my purse; a safety pin earring Lea's first boyfriend gave her before she let him feel her up for the first time; a pair of yellow sunglasses I bought with my babysitting money. Nothing important. Nothing that we couldn't live without, but it was amusing. Lea and I had something that set us apart from everyone else. It made us different. Interesting.

We would end up at the empty lot, and Beth would sit next to the hole and presto, just like magic, whatever item we'd been searching for would emerge clutched in her fist.

"She's stealing that shit. Trying to convince us she's special," Lea said after the second time.

"I don't think so. She's never excited when she finds something. Or proud of herself. If anything, she looks ashamed. Like she's just done something dirty."

"Uh. Yeah. She stole our stuff."

We hid random things in secret places: in shoe boxes in the backs of our closets, stuffed down garbage disposals, thrown into the woods on our way to school, eyes closed. We didn't tell each other where they were, but when we told Beth about what we had lost, she would lead us to the lot, put her hand in the hole, and pull out each and every trinket.

I'm not sure if she knew that we were using her. If she understood that was the only reason we let her hang around. Because she could find lost things and bring them home again like our own personal magic trick.

We liked to think that we were doing her a favor. That without us, she'd languish in social hell. No friends. No one to talk to. We adopted her because it amused us. We curled her hair to see if we could, put coral lipstick and liquid eyeliner on her as if she were a doll, and then gave her the crumbs of our affection. Still, she smiled at us and took us down to the lot when we had something that needed finding.

━━

"DON'T ASK Beth to come. She gives me the creeps when we have boys with us. The way she sits there and stares. Like she's never seen a pair of tits before," Lea said.

"Maybe don't pull your tits out then," I said, and she flipped me the bird.

Lea and I were in love with the feel of warm hands against the small of our backs and the musty scent of Acqua Di Gio, and the boys who had lied to us could give us both. We were going to meet them down at the lot.

I can't remember the boys' names—they were generic, Chris or Mark or James. What I do remember is a swoop of strawberry blond hair, freckles, green eyes. Hands in my hair and on my waist. Laughter. Someone brought a radio and Pearl Jam was singing in the background about last kisses. Everything moving in slow motion, like a dream. Beth somewhere in the background, humming along.

When the other boy, Lea's boy, started screaming, I thought I had fallen asleep, slipped into the half shadow world of nightmare. Beth stood beside him, her arms cradling something I couldn't see, and the boy screamed again.

"What the fuck? What the fuck?" He scrambled backwards.

"I'm sorry," Beth said and extended her arms outward, offered him whatever she held.

"Please. I thought I could do it. I could feel him. Down there in the dark," Beth said, and the boy recoiled.

"Get her the fuck away from me," he said, but no one moved.

"Beth," Lea said and reached out for her, but she turned away, clutched the thing in her arms to her chest.

"I'm sorry. I thought I could bring him back for you. You

miss him so much. I can feel it," she said, and I saw what she carried. The rotting body of a small, white dog rested in her arms. Eyes glassed over like two dark marbles.

If the boys ran, I don't remember. There was only Beth, sobbing, her fingers tangled in the dog's white fur. It took two hours to get her to let go of it, to convince her to bury it under a pile of dead leaves, and get her on her feet.

We took her home; walked under moonlight that turned Beth's hair silver, the streaks of mud on her fingers into ink. I don't ever remember her as beautiful, but that night, her beauty was a terrible thing.

"What did you do?" I said when we got to her porch. Her eyes were translucent. It was like looking through glass into something with no bottom.

"Father made me a door," she said.

"What do you mean?"

"She's there. Behind the door. But I can't open it completely. Not yet," Beth said and disappeared into the gloom of the house.

That night I dreamed of Beth. She crawled out from between my legs, her fingernails digging against my thighs.

<hr>

WE NEVER TALKED about the night with the dog. That year, when something went missing, Lea and I let it go. Didn't wonder about where it had gone or tear apart our rooms searching. The lot and the things we did there faded into the myths of our childhood.

I was going to New Orleans for school that fall. Lea was headed to Atlanta to chase a bass player in a shitty rock band. "He's really good, Willa. They're going to make it. You'll see."

Beth was going to stay home. Take care of her father.

"He's sick," she said, but she never told us with what. Only that she had to help him. The idea of her in that house, alone with her father—a man I'd never seen—nauseated me.

"You need to be out. On your own. You know, *live*," I told her. The way she smiled at me—lips chewed open and bleeding —made my skin itch.

In three weeks, I'd be far away from all of it: from Beth, from the lot, from all the lost things she had found. From the nightmares that were coming more and more frequently. From the new fear curling hard and sharp in my belly.

Lea went home early. Her rock and roll boy had told her that he might drop by later. She wanted to be sure she shaved her legs in case he did.

One by one, the partygoers stumbled out into the night, followed the moon back to their beds, until there was only Beth and me.

"Walk me home?" she asked.

I don't remember getting up to leave, my feet falling into the familiar path to Beth's house. Right onto Lakshire, left on Hope Circle, left again onto Cumberland Way. We were standing on her porch, when I realized that I had dropped out for a bit. I dismissed the lost time as being more than a little drunk.

Beth turned to me, took my hand, and opened her front door.

"Come inside," she said, and I hesitated, my foot brushing against the threshold. Warm air pressed against my face, heavy with something that smelled like yeast, like bread baking.

"I shouldn't," I said.

"It's okay." Her hand was hot over mine, and she pulled me inside. "I want to show you something."

The door closed.

"I want you to meet my father. He'll be so happy to see you again. It's been so long," she said, and I wanted to tell her she was mistaken, that I had never met her father, but my tongue was heavy and her hand pulled me into the dark.

"This way."

She led me into a hallway. Pictures lined the walls. A series of Beth at various ages, her hands and arms covered in dirt as she offered them to whomever stood behind the camera. In some she was smiling, her teeth long and wolfish. In others, she looked down, her hair covering her face.

"We'll go through the door. And then everything will be fine. Like it was before. Before everything was lost."

Beneath our feet, the carpet had given way to hard packed dirt, the walls covered with moss. A man stood at the end of the hallway facing a door, his back to us. Dark hair streaked with silver, clipped short. A white shirt tucked into jeans.

"This is my father," she said, dropping my hand. The man turned, bending to place a kiss on his daughter's lips. When she opened her mouth to him, I tried to turn away, tried not to hear Beth moan, but my arms felt heavy and would not move to cover my ears.

Beth paused before the door, her hand pressed against the wood.

"You always were my favorite, Willa. Will you help us? Will you help me find something that we lost?" Beth opened the door.

The doorway opened into Harper's old lot. We were *inside* the hole, the one where Beth found lost things, looking out and up into the night sky. No moon. No stars. Only the sound of something vast moving just beyond the hole. Something dragging itself along dirt paths.

"He made me a door. And I went searching. Hands seeking in the dark. Looking for what we lost. It took a long time, but I found her. She was so small. So quiet. Curled up like a cat at the bottom of a well," Beth said, and her father took her hand.

My mouth tasted of blood, sweet and hot and full of iron.

"Who did you find?" I asked, but she didn't answer.

Beth went down on her belly with her father behind her. They crawled up, up, up and through the hole and into the night, leaving me behind.

Whatever crawled along in the dirt laughed.

"Mother. We found you," she said, and I closed my eyes.

We bury our dead in the ground. We tend to the seeds and water them with our tears. We wait and watch. Sometimes, what we find is beautiful. Other times, all of the hope we put inside the seeds rots and decays. Then, we mourn all we have lost. The things we can never find. What we have thrown into the woods with our eyes closed.

The next morning, I woke up in my bed with no memory of how I got there and the fuzzy leftovers of a champagne headache. My thighs burned, as if someone had clawed their way out of me, but there were no scratches. No blood.

Three weeks later, I boarded an airplane for New Orleans. Neither I nor Lea heard from Beth after the night of the party.

Over the next three years, Lea and I drifted apart and came together with the strange consistency of childhood friends. We called each other when the men next to us were sleeping, and we whispered the lies that we had rehearsed, the fabricated stories we'd adopted to keep ourselves sane. If Lea had her own secrets to keep, I didn't ask, and she never asked me either.

"I dream about her," Lea said.

"Me, too."

"I called her house once. About a year ago. A woman answered. Said that she was Beth's mother, but her mother died. Didn't she? I think about her, but everything blurs together, and I can't be sure if what I'm remembering is real," Lea said. We didn't have to say that we were afraid.

Neither of us went back home. Out mothers begged us to visit, but we came up with reasons to stay away. Finals to study for. A new job that wouldn't give us the time off. A cold that I just couldn't shake. If Beth even still lived there, we didn't know. We didn't ask our mothers, and they never mentioned it. It was like she had never existed—a ghost.

Eventually, I convinced myself I had dreamed that night, down in the hole, with the stars so clear, but every couple of months, I would wake to the taste of dirt in my teeth and Beth's voice in my ear, her nails digging into my thighs.

It took twenty years for me to come home.

―――

TERRIN WAS four when we lost him. An accident. Sun in the eyes of the driver behind us. Didn't see the brake lights. No one's fault.

Five months went by, and I could not move. Could not speak. Vasily packed his things. In the story I tell myself, he kissed me when he left.

"Come home, Willa," my mother said over the phone. She sounded like an old woman, and I thought of what it would be like to bury her. It would feel right. Not like the world had just slipped inside out.

"Did Beth move away?" I asked her, but I knew the answer.

"Who? Oh, *Beth*. I see her every now and then at the store with her mother and father. She takes care of them I think. Always was a strange girl."

I went home and slept in my mother's house. It was no longer mine. There was a bed that she kept, but the girl who had slept there was not me.

Lea came. Took a red eye in from Charleston. My mother let her into the bedroom, and Lea sat on the edge of the mattress, picked at a loose thread. Neither of us spoke, and she went away when the sun began to set, told me that she loved me, that she would be back.

I slept, and I dreamed of a little boy with dark hair like his father, a small hand curled in mine, the sound of his laughter. I waited. I spoke his name and hers into the silence.

It took nine days for Beth to come to me. I woke up to her crouched on the bed. Her feet were dirty, and she'd left dark streaks on the white quilt.

"Can you still find lost things?" I said. She took my hand,

and I followed her out the door, down the streets I memorized as a girl and then followed when I was a teenager.

The lot had not changed. Broken bottles, cigarette butts, and candy wrappers still tangled in the grass. The ghosts of two girls and a third who came to them, who brought them nightmares. And somewhere in all of that, a door.

"There's. more than death in the ground, Willa," she said and knelt down.

"Yes," I said, and watched as she reached beneath the earth and pulled.

Acknowledgments

These stories would not exist without a myriad of people. Damien Angelica Walters has offered constant feedback and encouragement and without her input much of my writing would not exist. Michael Wehunt is an invaluable resource and a writer who is so good in his own right I don't actually know how I'm able to be friends with him instead of living in constant jealousy.

A huge thank you to the editors who published these stories in their magazines: Elise Tobler, CM Muller, Scott R. Jones, Paul Michael Anderson, Justin Steele, Laird Barron, Kelly Abbott, Jonathan Laden, Andrew S. Fuller, Simon Strantzas, Michael Kelly, Ken Wood, Sam Cowan, Jacob Haddon, Andy Cox, and Sebastian Rudolph. Many thanks to Ken Wood and John Boden of *Shock Totem* for being there at the beginning and seeing something in my little book.

A huge thanks to Jason Sizemore and Lesley Connor for their dedication to the collection.

A million thanks to Mikio Murakami for the beautiful artwork; somehow, my vision made it onto paper, and for that I cannot express my gratitude.

Thanks to Paul Tremblay, S.P. Miskowski, Richard Thomas, and Simon Strantzas for their exceedingly kind words about the stories here.

To anyone who has offered me a kind word, advice, or encouragement while on this journey, I so value your place in my life. For my friends and family who know what I'm doing when I disappear behind my computer screen, thank you for giving me the time and space to let these stories out of my head. I love you all.

About the Author

Kristi DeMeester is the author of *Beneath*, a novel published by Word Horde. Her short fiction has been reprinted or appeared in Ellen Datlow's *The Best Horror of the Year Volume 9*, *Year's Best Weird Fiction* Volumes 1 and 3, in addition to publications such as *Black Static*, *Apex*, and several others. In her spare time, she alternates between telling people how to pronounce her last name and how to spell her first. This is her first short fiction collection.

www.kristidemeester.com

SING ME YOUR SCARS

APEX VOICES BOOK #03

In her first collection of short fiction, Damien Walters weaves her lyrical voice through suffering and sorrow, teasing out the truth and discovering hope.

BY DAMIEN ANGELICA WALTERS

"*Sing Me Your Scars* revolves in the mind's eye in a kaleidoscope of darkness and wonder."
Laird Barron, author of *The Croning* and *The Beautiful Thing That Awaits Us All*

"Anatomies of dreams and nightmares, Walters is a writer to watch."
John Langan, author of *The Wide, Carnivorous Sky and Other Monstrous Geographies*

ISBN: 978-1-937009-28-1 ~ ApexBookCompany.com